Blood Memories

ORDER OF THE DRAGON - BOOK II

ALLISON A. ANDREWS

AAW PUBLISHING

To the BookTok and Bookstagram communities for supporting Indie Authors and making reading cool again!

Contents

Song List

Dynasty – MIIA

How Villains Are Made – Madalen Duke

Raise Up The Lights – League of Legends, The Seige

White Flag – Bishop Briggs

Human – Rag'n'Bone Man

...Ready for It? – Taylor Swift

I Didn't Ask For This – Beth Crowley

Redemption – Besomorph, Coopex, RIELL

In A Perfect World – Dean Lewis, Julia Michaels

I Wish You Cheated – Alexander Stewart

Six Feet Under – Oshins, Leslie Powell

Born To Die – Euphoria, Bolshiee

Up In Flames – Ruelle

I Don't Want To Watch The World End With Someone Else
– Clinton Kane

Prologue

UNTIL A YEAR AGO, I had led what you would call a normal life. Boring even. I'd always done everything that was expected of me - getting good grades at school, attending a good University, and finding a man who loved and wanted to marry me.

All of that changed when my fiance, Will, was murdered in front of me.

By a vampire.

I discovered that I was part of a secret organisation, the Order of the Dragon, which had been formed to keep the reality of the world's darkness from the human race.

Will returned from the dead, hell-bent on also turning me into a vampire.

I was informed that it was my destiny to end a war waged for centuries between two different races of vampires, daywalkers and nightwalkers.

Oh, and I fell in love with a daywalker who was closer to six hundred than my own ripe age of twenty-five.

But none of that compared to what happened last week.

My lover's identical twin brother, along with my own identical twin sister, had taken it upon themselves to attempt to turn me into one of them—a nightwalker.

And because of a promise I had extracted from Liam, the love of my life, was forced to take matters into his own hands, hoping that when I woke up, I wouldn't be on the wrong side of this war.

I've begun to realise that the world's reality is not as simple as discerning good from evil.

Sleeping Beauty had it easy. After True Love's kiss, she woke to the sight of Prince Charming and happily ever after.

I woke up to find my prince charming was keeping secrets, and the world sucked.

Welcome to reality.

Chapter One

THE SMELL SURROUNDED ME and blocked out all my other senses. Once I could get past the assault that smelled of rotting fruit, sewerage and a mixture of men's and women's cologne, I opened my eyes to take in my surroundings. I felt like I was pushing through a dense fog, cloying at every part of my body as if holding me back in the dark.

My brain was a jumbled mess of thoughts, and I had no idea where I was. Or even who I was, for that matter. All I could do was look around me in wonder, noticing the spider's web in the corner in great detail. I was able to make out the tiny hairs on the legs of the spider that spun its web with ease.

The room I was in was lavishly furnished. I lay on a giant four-poster bed with rich burgundy hangings. Two antique oil lamps made of a mosaic of ornate-coloured glass on both bedside tables burned brightly in the darkness.

The window was open, allowing a breeze to enter the room, laced with the faintest trace of the ocean and the other scents that continued to lay siege upon my senses.

I sat up quickly and walked to the window, looking outside as I attempted to make sense of my current situation.

Where am I?

The view was breathtaking. Although the moon was high in the sky, I could make out every single detail. The stars twinkled in a way I had never seen before. I could see a river that ran fast and strong, with debris strewn through it, items that appeared to be pontoons with... I looked closer... Yep, that was a jetski on top of that pontoon.

What was going on? I couldn't recognise anything about my surroundings. Who am I? My thoughts were all over the place, and none made sense. I couldn't even remember my name, let alone how I got here, or where *here* even was...

"You're safe," a voice said from behind me. I turned quickly, backing up against the wall next to the window, staring at the man standing in the doorway. In one hand, he held a ceramic jug, in the other an empty glass, and he wore an expression that was a mixture of concern and relief.

I stared at him, taking in everything about him. He was familiar, yet I had no idea who he was. He was incredibly handsome, with a well-built, lean body and thick, brown hair that was so dark it was almost black. His piercing blue eyes were intense while he ran his gaze over every inch of me.

"I know you're confused at the moment. It will all come back to you soon. But you're safe here. You're with me. Liam..." His words trailed off, and somewhere within my mind, I knew that the name meant something to me. That *he* meant something to me.

He cautiously entered the room fully, placing the jug and glass on the bedside table. He moved towards me slowly, keeping his hands where I could see them. I watched him from where I remained pressed against the wall, still uncertain of everything.

"Isolde... I'm not going to hurt you."

Isolde... the name rang in my ears. A whisper of a memory pushed at my mind, pressing to be let in amongst all the other thoughts bouncing around inside my brain. He stopped in front of me, so close that I was forced to lift my face to look up at him.

He touched the side of my face softly, and the familiarity of his touch quickly squashed the urge to pull away, and a memory rushed to the surface. A memory of us standing exactly how we were now, my back against a wall, his face close to mine. With his fingers tangled in my hair and the need to be close to him. To be kissing him.

I gave in to that need now, wrapping my arms around his neck and pulling him closer while I reached to kiss him. He resisted briefly before relaxing into it, pulling me tight against him while he deepened the kiss, a hand tangled in my hair. His other hand moved across the small of my back, his fingers running lightly along the waistband of my jeans with such familiarity that I knew we'd perfected this.

The need to be closer to him grew more urgent, and I pulled him closer. His mouth moved away from mine to begin kissing my neck. As his lips pressed into my neck, another memory surfaced of his teeth sinking into my skin and the ecstasy of his bite. I moaned his name, gripping his shoulders as my memories came flooding back.

Liam pulled away and looked me in the eye.

"What do you remember?" He asked, and I could feel tears starting to form in the corners of my eyes.

"Everything," I whispered, my voice shaking.

He began firing off questions rapidly, gripping my shoulders tightly.

"Who are you?"

"Isolde Smith."

"Where are you from?"

"Brisbane... Australia."

"Who am I?"

"You're Liam—my boyfriend. Well, I guess you're my boyfriend. Boyfriend seems like a weird word for a five-hundred-year-old," I said with a small smile, but he wasn't ready to joke around yet.

"What else do you remember?"

I paused to gather my thoughts, looking at a spot on the wall as I worked through the fog as memories clicked into place.

"You have a twin brother, Connor, who is a nightwalker and one of the people responsible for my sister being turned," I said, pushing aside the pain that this memory caused.

Liam's jaw clenched before he slowly nodded.

"And they both tried to turn me into a nightwalker... But you saved me... Right?"

Liam froze then, and I knew I was missing something vital.

"Liam, what happened? Where are we? What am I?" My voice wavered, and I looked into his eyes again. "You didn't save me, did you? Or you tried... The last thing I remember is you saying you were sorry, more pain and then the sound of a car crash..."

The sadness in his eyes confirmed this, and I began to shake.

"I... I couldn't stop the change... You were already so far gone... I didn't know what you would be like when you woke up...." His voice was unsteady, and he brought his hand to my cheek.

Something else occurred to me.

"Can't you hear my thoughts?" I asked.

One of Liam's abilities was to read the thoughts of those around him. He often tried not to, in attempts to avoid invading the privacy of others, but he had always been in tune with me. The day before my abduction, I had begun to be able to hear his thoughts within my mind, having formed a spiritual bond with him.

My stomach dropped when I noticed I could no longer hear him either.

"I'm sure it'll come back...." His tone didn't give me much confidence that he genuinely believed that.

I pushed aside a burning sensation at the back of my throat.

"So that means...."

"You're a vampire, Isolde," a voice said, and Liam scowled, spinning to face the woman who entered the room behind him. She was petite, at least a foot shorter than myself, with long black hair and the striking blue eyes that each vampire had. She was beautiful, and her voice had a slight accent that I couldn't place.

"Eve," I whispered.

Although Liam had never spoken of her to me, I already knew who she was, though I didn't remember ever having met her. My emotions were swirling, and I could feel myself growing more on edge with each step that brought her closer to me. Liam stood before me, perhaps to keep the distance between us.

"You know who I am, don't you, Isolde?" Her voice was sultry, and there was something incredibly sexy about her. I'd never been attracted to women before, but something about her drew me in. Although there was nothing particularly threatening in her appearance, I could feel the magic surrounding her, and everything inside me screamed that she was incredibly powerful.

"How... How do I know you?" I attempted to step around Liam, but he put his arm out in front of me, forcing me to stay behind him while looking at her over his shoulder.

"Your mind will eventually begin to clear." She said with a shrug, not giving anything away.

I was growing frustrated by her nonchalance and Liam's defensive stance in front of me. I pushed against him, expecting some resistance, but was surprised when he moved aside, giving in quicker than he had ever done in the past. It was a moment before I remembered I had increased strength now, and he had moved more out of necessity than having given up.

I stood beside him as a fourth person entered the room. He was around the same height as Liam, though he was stockier. He had blonde hair and appeared a little rough around the edges, although I was more than sure that

Liam could hold his own against this man should it come down to it.

That he was also a vampire was obvious, given the company he kept, but I felt the same familiarity with him as I did with Eve.

"Ronson," I said his name quietly, and the look Liam gave me out of the corner of my eye confirmed that I was correct.

"OK, seeing as no one appears to want to tell me how I know you two, can someone please explain where I am and what is going on?" I demanded, becoming aware of the change in my voice for the first time. I had always had a reasonably low voice, but now it sounded deeper, throatier.

"You are in my home," Eve replied, opening her arms wide while watching me intently. There didn't appear to be anything inviting about how she was looking at me. It was almost like being a bird in a cage with the family cat sitting across the room, flicking its tail from side to side as it worked out how best to get the bird out of the cage and into its mouth. Ronson's face held the same look, and I felt Liam tense up beside me, his hand reaching out to pull me behind him again. Despite the power I could feel surrounding Eve, I refused to allow myself to be intimidated by either of them, seeing as I had no idea what they believed I would do. I wrapped my hand around Liam's wrist and shook my head at him.

"And where exactly might that be? Are we still in Brisbane?" I directed this question at Liam, who nodded but never took his eyes off the others, his jaw clenched.

"A lot has happened whilst you were sleeping, Isolde."
Eve gestured towards the window beside me, and I looked
outside once more at the raging river.

"That's the Brisbane River? But I don't understand...
I have never seen the River flow like that, and it is so
high...." I watched a huge tree float past, the current forcing it to move quicker than I ever thought possible.

"The day that you were turned, the floods started,"
Ronson stated, speaking for the first time. He struck me
as the silent type, speaking only when necessary.

"Everything has started now," Eve added.

I had no idea what she meant by that statement, and
the way that Liam clenched his jaw next to me made it
clear that he wasn't impressed with how this little meet
and greet was going.

"I think you should leave now. Give Isolde time to adjust." Liam stepped forward and stared them both down.
Eve watched me for a moment more before finally turning
and indicating for Ronson to follow her. He shut the door
behind him, and Liam turned to face me again.

"I don't understand anything that just happened," I
said. The mess in my mind was starting to become beyond
frustrating. I felt like I needed to shake my head to get the
chaotic thoughts back into some order, but I knew that
would be a useless effort.

I turned to the window, leaning against the frame, and
stared into the darkness again. Liam came to stand beside
me and pressed his hand lightly on the small of my back. I
sensed he needed to touch me to ensure I was truly there.

"Where are we, Liam? I know we are in Eve's house,
but where exactly is that? Nothing looks familiar," I said
quietly. The fact that the river appeared to be taking over

the city I loved probably wasn't helping me recognise any landmarks.

"We're in West End. Eve and Ronson set up residence here shortly after the Order did." I knew he meant that they moved here when I was born, and everything started to change. I turned to face him, leaning my hip against the window ledge. His hand moved, resting gently against my opposite hip.

"So they know about the prophecy? And what exactly is their part in all of this? What happened when I blacked out? I remember hearing a car crash." Liam reached up to push my hair off my face with his free hand, his eyes glistening a little as he took a deep breath.

"When I held you in my arms, all I could hear was your voice begging me not to let you become a nightwalker. To drain the blood out of you - what was left of it - was the hardest thing I've ever done, but you were going to die, and I couldn't let that happen. I couldn't let you become one of them. I couldn't lose you." He let out a ragged breath, and I slid my hand up to rest over his heart. "And then we were hit, and someone knocked me out and tore you from my arms. When I woke up, we were here, and Eve told me that it was her and Ronson that took us, that took you from my arms, and I didn't know if I'd succeeded in keeping you from the darkness. I've spent the past week watching over you, not knowing if you would wake up with evil inside you. To have you standing here in front of me like this, to know that I was able to save you, you have no idea of the relief I feel right now." His voice was thick as he pulled me to him and hugged me close.

I pressed my face into his chest, letting my tears stay hidden.

Because I didn't think he had saved me. Not really. I never wanted to be a vampire. Good or bad, this wasn't what I had ever wanted for myself. Although everything else within me was a confused mess, I was sure of that much. Feeling Liam's relief while he held me tightly filled me with guilt.

He pulled away slightly, lifting my chin and lowering his lips to mine. I let myself become lost in the sensation, the familiarity giving me a brief sense of comfort.

I felt myself sinking into his arms, but a memory that had been pushing at the back of my mind finally made its way through the chaos, and I was swept away to a place that I had never been before and yet knew so well...

Chapter Two

I GAZED INTO THE *firelight, attempting to process the information my mother had imparted earlier, when the sound of a booming knock on the front door caused me to jump. Who could be visiting at this time of night?*

I followed Callum to the door, standing back while the servant unbolted the lock and pulled the heavy oak doors open.

I was struck dumb momentarily, unable to take in the vision before me.

It couldn't be. It just wasn't possible. After all these months?

"Connor?" I asked quietly, staring as my twin brother stepped across the threshold. He was accompanied by another man, both dressed in travelling clothes and wrapped in cloaks to protect themselves from the bitter cold.

"Hello, brother." Connor smiled, and I rushed forward to hug him fiercely, relief flooding through my veins. Pulling away from me, Connor continued to smile, turning to look

back at his companion, who was still lingering on the stone steps.

"Liam, why don't you invite my companion in, out of the cold?" While the request was odd, I knew it would be bad manners to expect anyone, even a stranger, to remain outside on such a bitterly cold evening.

"Of course, of course. Please come in. Any friend of Connor's is welcome here." I said, indicating to Callum to take their coats. Callum stood frozen, the door handle still gripped in his hand. I clapped my hands while Connor's companion stepped through the doorway, causing Callum to jump to attention.

"Callum, take their coats," I commanded, embarrassed, but Connor waved Callum's misstep aside.

"Callum, old man. It is so good to see you," Connor said. Callum stared at him open-mouthed, only answering once I'd cleared my throat.

"And you too, Master Connor." Callum's voice trembled slightly, and I knew I would need to speak with him about his strange behaviour later. I led the way back into the sitting room while Callum hurried off to fetch our mother, along with some tea to warm our guests.

Once seated before the fire, I gazed at my brother in wonder.

"Connor. Where have you been all these months? Father sent men out everywhere searching for you." I found something about the smile on my brother's face unnerving, although I could not put a finger on it. His companion continued to sit silently. His presence was off-putting while he looked around the room with a sneer.

"I apologise for the worry my absence has caused everyone. I've been off on a remarkable adventure," Connor said, *his voice taking on an almost dream-like quality. I didn't know what to make of him. He appeared the same, but everything about his demeanour had changed... Although, upon closer inspection, I realised not everything about his appearance was the same. His eyes, once the same green-blue as mine, were now a piercing, almost glowing, blue. Not only that, there was something else in them that I could not identify.*

I began to feel nervous while Connor continued to avoid answering my questions about his whereabouts, instead making polite conversation whilst looking around the room, clearly noting the changes I had made since our father's passing. He never asked about our father, leading me to believe he knew he had passed and did not care for specifics. His gaze fell on the stand in the corner where my Bible lay open, and he seemed to be resisting the urge to say something about its presence, which I found odd. He had always respected my devotion to the Lord. Like I had overlooked his dalliances with whichever woman he was courting at the time.

I shook myself from my musings, looking up to see our mother run into the room in a most unladylike manner. She came to an abrupt halt just inside the door, staring at Connor. Unlike the joy I had expected, something else was written on her face.

"Connor, is it really you?" She whispered, her brown hair escaping from under her nightcap in wisps, making her appear dishevelled.

"Hello, Mother." Connor rose to his feet and moved towards her, his arms outstretched. She stepped back, and I noted her expression was the same one that had appeared on

Callum's face. I could not see Connor's face, but I assumed he still wore his eerily pleasant smile.

"Stay back. I know what you are." Mother's voice was forceful and took me by surprise.

"What am I? Mother, it is me, your son. I am Connor." Though he still had his back to me, his voice became mocking, and I raised an eyebrow.

"Connor is dead. You are a demon!" She screamed, backing out of the room before fleeing down the long hallway. I stared after her.

"Demon? What is she talking about, Connor?" I demanded.

Connor turned around abruptly, but it was to his companion that he directed his following words.

"Keep him here!" He commanded, and the man grabbed me so quickly it was as if he had been standing right behind me instead of across the room.

"What are you doing?! Unhand me this instant!" I struggled to free myself, but the man, who appeared to have brute strength on his side, was far stronger than myself, a man who had dedicated his life to books. Connor had left the room in pursuit of our mother. The man held me in his vice-like grip, and I heard her scream. I pictured her cowering while Connor stalked her through the house.

Eventually, he reappeared, dragging our mother behind him, his arm clasped around her chest and shoulders while she struggled against him.

"What are you doing?!" I exclaimed. My assailant released his hold, tossing me roughly aside and moving back to Connor's side. My head hit the wall hard, and pain shot through my body. Connor threw our mother down on the chaise in the corner, and his companion moved forward

to pin our mother in place. I was amazed at his strength, watching him while he held her still with only one hand. Connor's face remained twisted into the strange smile that sent chills down my spine as he leaned closer to her.

"Mother, that is no way to greet your long-lost son," he said, admonishing our mother, and despite myself, I gasped when she spat in his face.

"You are no son of mine! I know what you are!" She yelled, continuing in her attempt to break free. Connor casually wiped her spittle off his face with a handkerchief.

"Connor! I demand you tell me at once what is going on here! Why are you doing this?!" I hoped my voice sounded more commanding than I felt.

His smile was now fixed upon me, and I shuddered involuntarily. Mother's words from the night before came flooding back to me.

"You're a vampire?" I whispered, the fear beginning to rise within me.

How could this be true?

I struggled to get to my feet, but nausea rolled through me, dizziness overpowering me from the knock I'd taken to my head.

"Ah, so she's finally told you about your birthright." Connor grinned at our mother, watching her struggle to push his companion off. "It's about time, woman. Although I admit his ignorance and disbelief made all of this go according to plan, thank you for standing by your misguided loyalty to the precious Order. It's been most helpful."

"Do not speak to her that way! She is your mother - you owe her your respect!" Years of good breeding overcame my terror at what my brother had become. For his part, Connor

simply laughed once again. He turned back in my direction, and I recoiled when he stalked towards me.

"Oh, Liam, you make this too easy! It's quite sad how determined you are to stick to your closed-minded views. But where is your precious God now? Why has he not struck me down before I rip your throats out?" He looked up at the ceiling, taunting the Almighty, before fixing his gaze on me. "I'll tell you why, my sweet, innocent little brother." His eyes turned feral. "Because he does not exist! He is nothing but a fairy tale!"

"Blasphemy! How can you dare say such things?" I cried. Both men laughed together this time.

"You always were such a good little boy, Liam. But so naive. So convinced you were right, yet so misguided. God is a being that was created from the minds of men in an attempt to find something to comfort themselves when the darkness of the world engulfed them. But I know the truth. I am a God! I have died and risen once more, like your precious Jesus." He taunted.

I attempted to block him out while I crossed myself to fight off his influence. I prayed silently, begging the saints to intercede to save me from the evil before me. God would hear me. He would not abandon me to this demon that now wore my brother's flesh. Connor's lips twisted into a cruel smile, watching my lips move in silent prayer.

"Pray away, dear brother. It will not save you. It did not save me. And it will not save our mother." He looked back as his companion reached down with his free hand and wrenched her head to the side, exposing her neck. Connor wrapped his arms around me, keeping me from moving so much as an inch. She screamed and attempted to push him off of her, but it was no use, and he sank his teeth

into her neck. I was forced to watch while the monster brutally drained the life out of our mother. Her face was turned towards me, and tears streamed down my face while I watched the colour drain away, her eyes turning glassy before eventually losing all signs of life.

I stared, incapable of sound, while the creature ripped her head from her shoulders in one brutal movement. He dropped her body to the ground, blood running onto the floor while he straightened and turned towards me.

"No! Stay away from me!" I struggled against Connor, and he tightened his already painful grip. His companion smiled.

"Ah, brother... I truly have missed you... I can't wait for you to join me," Connor whispered in my ear. His companion stepped closer, taking my face in his hands and looking directly into my eyes.

"It will only hurt for a moment... And when you awaken, you will be just like your brother and be free for all eternity," the vampire spoke for the first time.

I stared into his eyes, the reality of my situation dawning on me. He hadn't come here to kill me. He wanted me to join him and my brother. To become a monster like them.

He gripped my hair and yanked my head to the side. But, when he lowered his mouth to my throat, a loud noise outside caused him to pause. He wiped our mother's blood from his lips, casting a look at the window over his shoulder.

His surprised expression drew my attention to the window, and I felt Connor's arms loosen their grip on me. Callum stood on the other side of the glass, crossbow in hand, his silhouette lit up by the crowd of people standing behind him, each holding a flaming torch.

A mob of vigilantes.

Connor swore under his breath while the sound of breaking glass echoed through the room.

Callum was not a good shot, missing the vampire's heart, though the crossbow bolt grazed his arm. Connor let me go, and I fell to the floor, falling into the blood pooling at our mother's headless torso. A torch was thrown through the broken window, and the vampire looked down at me momentarily before fleeing from the room. I struggled to my feet, trying to avoid the flames, and my whole body began to shake. Connor paused in his escape, staring back at me from the doorway. I could hear the yells of the mob, and some part of me knew that they would turn on me next. With a final, almost sad look, Connor turned and fled, and I stumbled out of the room through the opposite door, exiting the house through the servant's quarters. The mob had not yet reached the back of the manor, and I started running towards the woods bordering our property.

I ran for as long as possible, losing track of where I was and feeling lightheaded from the pain radiating from my head. Eventually, I came across what looked like an old, abandoned church. I had no memory of any church in the area, though I was grateful for its presence now as I collapsed on what was left of the altar. Exhausted and dizzy, I closed my eyes to keep the world from spinning above me.

A noise caused me to open my eyes, and I realised I was not alone. I looked up to find a woman standing over me. In my confused state, I couldn't quite understand what her expression meant, the pain in my head becoming more intense.

"You're injured." It wasn't a question, though I couldn't have answered her anyway, as I was too exhausted and weak. I could feel sleep taking me, and I closed my eyes.

I felt a sharp pain in my neck, and the world slowly turned black.

Chapter Three

THE FOG IN MY brain lifted, and I was back in Liam's embrace.

"You just saw one of my memories, didn't you? What was it?" His eyes searched mine while I struggled to comprehend what I had just seen. I shook my head slightly, and he tightened his grip briefly before stepping back.

"Well... Now I know why Eve looks so familiar... she was your sire...." I whispered, and Liam's eyes widened, hesitating before nodding slowly. I let out a long exhale, piecing myself back together.

"What was the memory?" He asked again. I tried not to read anything into the wariness that was evident in his voice. As though there were things in his past that he was concerned about me seeing...

"It was the night Connor and Adam showed up at your door," I said, returning to the bed to sit down.

Liam stayed where he was, looking down at me as I stared at my hands, trying to shake off the memory and return to reality, to myself, rather than seeing the world through his eyes. It was surreal to have someone else's memories running through your mind like they were your own. I was not fond of it. Would I eventually lose myself while I blended more with Liam? After all, I'd only been alive for twenty-five years, which was much less to remember than five hundred!

"You might have to be a bit more specific, seeing as, unfortunately, those two have shown up on my doorstep several times over the centuries, although all had similar outcomes...." His voice trailed off, and I saw that his face had taken on a distant expression while he became lost in the past.

"This was the first time. The night Adam killed your mother. The night you met Eve." Tears pricked at the corner of my eyes at the memory of watching my - well, Liam's - mother die. As if I was still there, and it had happened to me.

Liam sat beside me now, and I rested my head on his shoulder while he wrapped his arm around me, pulling me closer and kissing the top of my head.

"Is this what it's going to be like from now on? Remembering things from your past as if they happened to me?" The tears that slid silently down my cheeks were no longer for a long-dead woman but for the loss of yet another part of my world, the last vestiges of humanity that had now been ripped away from me.

"It eventually gets easier..." His voice was thick with emotion, and I knew that "eventually" would be a very long time.

"How do I stop myself from losing who I am... Or who I was?" I wanted to crawl into his lap so that he could wrap his arms around me and I could feel safe. But I stayed where I was, knowing that no matter where I was, safety would never be an option again.

"It's hard at first. But I'm going to help you. You're not alone, Isolde." He said, and I turned my face toward him and buried it in his chest, finally giving in to the sobs fighting to be released. He lifted me as easily as he would a child, and I ended up right where I'd wanted, in his lap, his arms around me, while I mourned everything I had lost.

I cried for what could have been minutes or hours. What was the point of keeping track of time when you suddenly had eternity ahead of you?

My sobs eventually lessened, and Liam held me close, running his hand up and down my back. His nearness still had the same effect on me that it had always had, and I was grateful for that small semblance of normalcy. I twisted slightly so that I was looking up into his eyes. There were so many emotions in his eyes, and I knew he was right there with me, ready to help where he could.

It was comforting to know that I would at least have someone who understood what I was going through, even if it had been centuries since he'd had to adjust to this life.

"I love you," he whispered against my lips, kissing me softly.

"I love you too." I deepened the kiss, reaching up to wrap my arms around his neck and pull him closer. It was like an emotional switch had been flipped within me. Where seconds ago I was filled with sorrow, I was now consumed with a burning desire to get as close as possible to Liam, to push aside everything else and concentrate on nothing but being able to touch him and have him touch me.

His hands gripped my hips when I straddled his lap, trying to ignore the burning at the back of my throat, which had grown steadily more insistent since I opened my eyes.

Liam began moving his lips along my jaw, and I tilted my head back to allow him access to my throat, closing my eyes and attempting to focus only on his lips. On his hands and the effect they were having on my body. But the burning wouldn't cease. My gaze drifted over his shoulder to the jug and glass that he had placed on the bedside table when he'd first entered the room.

Sensing the shift in my focus, Liam pulled back to look at my face, then turned over his shoulder towards where I was looking, cursing softly under his breath.

"You need to feed." He said, but I shook my head quickly.

"No, I don't want to stop. Just keep kissing me, please?" I begged softly, not ready to deal with it all. Liam hesitated momentarily, nodding slowly before pulling me to him again. I tried desperately to lose myself once more to the sensation of his lips pressing to my skin just below my earlobe, and his hands continued holding my hips, pulling me further onto his lap. I drew his lips back to mine and kissed him fiercely while fighting the urge to surrender to the burning. But Liam slowly pulled back to look me in the eye. I was breathing heavily and trying with all my might not to look at the jug.

"Isolde, the more you try to fight it, the worse it will be. We need to get some blood into you. Now," he said, and I finally allowed him to slide me off his lap and get to his feet.

Although I still shook my head, I knew that he was right. I couldn't think of anything else while my throat burned like this.

He walked around the bed and began pouring the contents of the jug into the glass. The hunger kicked up another notch while I watched the thick, red liquid slide slowly down the side of the glass. I clenched my hands into fists to keep myself from launching off the bed and ripping the glass from his hands.

Once the glass was full, Liam brought it back to where I continued to sit, breathing heavily while I fought to maintain control. He handed me the glass, and although I was beyond hungry, I stared at the contents, fighting an internal war within myself. I knew that I needed to drink it to rid myself of the uncontrollable hunger, but the knowledge that I was about to ingest blood voluntarily was something I couldn't get past.

"Who's blood is this?" I stared at the glass while Liam watched me closely.

"It's animal blood," he replied. That didn't make me feel any better, and I imagined Eve killing a poor, defenceless animal to drain it of all its blood. I don't know why I assumed Eve had provided the blood - I guess I didn't want to think of Liam killing animals. Let alone the idea of him drinking from a human, even if that person willingly allowed it, as I had occasionally done for him.

I gave myself a mental shake and slowly brought the glass to my lips, resisting the urge to gag as I took my first mouthful. It still tasted like blood, but instead of being repulsed by it, it was the most fantastic thing I had ever tasted. I knew that it was still blood and the fact that I needed to drink it was wrong, but that didn't stop me from draining the glass before handing it back to Liam and requesting another.

Once my hunger had been appeased, the realisation of what I had just done hit me, and I found I wasn't in the mood to return to our previous activities. Liam lay down on the bed and pulled me to him. I curled up in a ball and cried silently while outside, people went about their lives, and I mourned the life I had lost.

Hours later, I pulled myself together enough to ask questions that hadn't occurred earlier.

"Where are my parents? Are they safe?" Because they had once shared a home with Aurora and me, their house was no longer safe because Aurora didn't need an invitation. And neither did I. Vampires required an invitation before they could enter the threshold of any new dwelling that housed humans, but they could still enter any home they had previously resided in.

This same strange magic was the reason why I'd had to sell the townhouse that Will and I had bought together (I'd eventually burned it to the ground after the next occupants were murdered and a nest of nightwalkers took up residence), and Aurora and I had rented our dream home, which had turned out to be a safe house for the Order of the Dragon.

"Yes. However, your house and theirs have a few feet of water through them. So they are staying with Briseis."

"And what do they know? About Aurora and I, I mean."

"You've been exchanging messages with them, and they think Aurora is still in Sydney," Liam said, and I studied his face for a moment, the meaning behind his words slowly sinking in.

"You mean someone from the Order has been impersonating me on the phone?" I wasn't sure how to feel about that, though I knew there wasn't any other way to keep my parents from freaking out and taking out a missing person's report on us. Liam nodded, and I cursed under my breath.

"What about Jacob? Where is he?" Aurora's boyfriend had also been living with us, and I suddenly wondered how exactly I would keep Aurora's death and current undead status from everyone we loved. And my own, for that matter. Although seeing that I wouldn't attempt to murder everyone, I figured my secret would be easier to keep.

"Jacob received a text message from Aurora's phone, breaking up with him, telling him that she was planning on staying in Sydney indefinitely."

"That's a bit harsh," I said with raised eyebrows.

"Harsh, but at least he'll be safe now. I spoke to him on the phone when he called, looking for you. He's pretty torn up. He packed up his stuff the day after everything happened and moved in with a friend for the time being, but he was talking about moving back to Townsville to get away from here." That's where Jacob had grown up and his family remained. I was saddened by the knowledge that I wouldn't see him anymore. He had been a good friend and a great boyfriend for Aurora. However, I had learned in the hours before my untimely demise that Aurora had been in love with Will. So, the knowledge that Jacob had escaped without learning the truth was a small comfort.

"What about Ainslie? Last time I saw her, the Order was going to perform a memory charm so that she didn't remember any of the stuff from the restaurant?" I asked. When she had seen my "dead" fiancé sitting just inches from her, my best friend of fifteen years had slightly freaked out, and Liam and I had been forced to tell her the truth, something that the Order tended to frown upon. But, given that I'd just seen my twin sister and realised she was now a nightwalker, I had lost all ability to give a crap what the Order wanted.

"Ainslie still knows everything we told her. Once she calmed down, Patrice talked with her, and Ainslie decided she wanted to join the Order." Liam said, and I raised an eyebrow. Although the Order had been made up of seventh daughters of seventh daughters and seventh sons of seventh sons, in recent years, with the size of families getting smaller, the Order had been forced to begin to allow civilians to join. Though they were kept in the dark about a large part of the organisation, they were called upon to help when more significant numbers were needed. They tended to be kept on a need-to-know basis, and none of them were told anything more than 'vampires are bad'. Although daywalkers tended not to be a threat to the general human population, Liam was the only one I knew of who worked side by side with the Order, and that was due to his history with them—from what I knew of his past, his time spent with the Order had caused others of his kind to steer clear. That is why he was the only daywalker I had met, although now I guess I could add Eve and Ronson to that list. If they were anything to go off, though, I wasn't sure I was ready to meet others. The idea that I was now one of them wasn't sitting well.

"I'm not sure I like the idea of Ainslie being involved with anything to do with the Order." I frowned, and Liam nodded.

"I know, I said as much to Patrice before everything turned to shit, but she pointed out that it was Ainslie's choice. She doesn't know about what has happened to you, though. The Order has been keeping tight-lipped about that." He ran a hand through his hair, and I noticed how exhausted he looked. This past week couldn't have been easy on him. He didn't require much sleep, but I sensed what little sleep he should have had eluded him while he struggled to keep my death from my family while anxiously waiting to see if I would wake up as an evil monster. I touched his face while he stared at the roof, forcing him to look at me while he continued lying on his back.

"Thank you for watching over me and caring for my friends and family." I kissed him softly before lying back down and allowing him to pull me close to his side again.

"I'd do it again in a heartbeat. I haven't seen anyone. It's all been over the phone. Although Eve and Ronson haven't technically been keeping me a prisoner here, there was no way in hell I was leaving you alone with them for even a second. I couldn't risk them disappearing with you to keep you away from the Order. I asked Gerard to leave a car nearby if I needed it." He gripped me tightly, and I could feel the tension in his body. I propped myself up on my elbow so that I could look at him once again.

"I'm here now. I'm not going anywhere. We'll sort out what we can - we always do. I love you. I'm realising now just how much I love you." I ran my fingers through his hair, and he closed his eyes briefly before pulling me down so that he could kiss me once more. I could feel his tension easing, and there was some desperation behind this kiss. His arms tightened around me, and I pushed every other thought aside, allowing myself to get lost in this moment with him, sighing while I sunk further into the kiss, and he wound his fingers through my hair. His other hand ran up and down my back under my shirt, his fingers lightly trailing a path along my spine, and I arched into his touch while he ran kisses down my throat.

"God, I missed you so much this last week. I don't know what I would have done if you had woken up as a nightwalker." His words were desperate, and I could hear the raw emotion in his whispered "I love you" when he rolled me onto my back and hovered over me, looking me over again. I saw the need in his eyes and raised my hand to his cheek. He leaned into my touch, closing his eyes, before turning to place a kiss on my palm. I moved to sit up, and he sat back, watching while I began peeling my clothes off frantically. He followed suit, and we were pressed together, skin to skin, holding each other close. I needed to feel every part of him against me. I needed him inside of me.

He moved down my body and used his tongue to trace a circle around my nipple while his hand worked its way between my legs. My back arched off the bed, his mouth and hand working in tandem. The sensation was like nothing I'd felt before when we were together, and I moaned, one hand clutching the sheet beside me while the other dug into his shoulder. My senses were heightened, and I could feel the orgasm building within seconds.

"God, Liam, please."

He moved faster, plunging two fingers inside me, rubbing my most sensitive spot firmly with his thumb and continued sucking hard on my breast until I exploded, crying out his name again.

Before I could breathe, he moved over and slid inside me with one fluid movement. I arched my back again and wrapped my legs around him tightly, drawing him in fully. I began rocking against him, urging him on while he hissed his approval and started moving with me.

"Tell me you love me," he growled, thrusting steadily, his eyes locked on mine.

"I love you." I moved my hips in time with his, and he groaned. I used that moment to flip us, rolling him onto his back and beginning to ride him, moving my hips while I ground down on him.

"Tell me you belong to me," I said, placing a hand on his throat, hips rolling faster until another orgasm began to build, even more powerful than before. He wrapped a hand around my wrist, using the other to guide my hips even faster, his gaze boring into mine.

"I'm yours, eternally fucking yours, Isolde. Now come apart for me." He moved his hand from my hip, and a single press with his finger just above where we were joined made me see stars again. He sat up to meet me when I collapsed into his arms. Gathering myself again, my forehead pressed to his shoulder while he guided my body to move up and down on him at a slower, more leisurely pace. I moaned, every movement overwhelming my senses.

Energy returning, I sat back up to look him in the eyes while I began rolling my hips again, and my gaze drifted to his throat. I wondered what it would be like to bite him like he had done with me in the past.

Taking one hand off my hip, he gripped my head, tangling his fingers in my hair, kissing me hard, stroking my tongue with his. I continued rolling my hips and gripped his face, needing to feel him against me.

He used his grip on my hair to pull my head back, and the protest I was about to utter died on my lips when he tilted his head. I hesitated, and he tightened his grip on my head, pushing me towards his exposed throat. I ran my tongue along my teeth, feeling how sharp my canines suddenly were, before placing my mouth on his skin. I bit down, and he moaned, gripping my hips and rocking me faster while I continued to feed as we worked closer and closer to orgasm.

"Fuck, Isolde."

I felt him tightening and began to move faster than I'd ever moved before, rocketing us both over the edge.

Our movements finally slowed, and we collapsed onto the bed together, arms wrapped firmly around one another. I pulled my mouth away and brought my lips to his before pressing our foreheads together while we fought to steady our breaths.

"I could get used to that." I smiled at his words and opened my mouth to answer him, but a rush of memories hit me, and I felt myself collapse down on him.

Chapter Four

I WATCHED HER MOVE *slowly from room to room, checking to make sure there was no one in the house with her. I had silently guarded this woman from the shadows ever since she was born, yet it was like seeing her for the first time tonight. She had grown into a truly stunning woman, and the confidence in every action showed that she was sure of herself. It saddened me to know that within weeks, that would all disappear once the nightmares kicked in, the visions and the knowledge that all was not right with the world.*

It had been so long since I had experienced the awakening, and I had only had a day of it. Isolde had months of it ahead of her until the Order could be sure she was ready. She had no idea that her entire world was about to change.

Will pulled up in his car and went inside. I witnessed their embrace at the front door and fought back the anger that was beginning to stir within me. I knew that Will had been seeing Aurora behind her back, attempting to experience the best of both worlds. I wished I could let Isolde know that the man she loved had, on occasion, spent time in another woman's arms. Her twin sister's arms.

But she didn't even know I existed. And so I remained silent, standing alone night after night, always in the dark, always on the edge of her life looking in.

The Order had so much invested in this woman that they had stopped viewing her as a person and saw only a being who needed to be prepared for the life they believed she was destined for.

I wanted to protect her from that so badly, yet I was powerless. My vampiric side stopped me from reaching the higher ranks of the Order. They were all trained to be wary of me, and I knew I was not truly one of them in the eyes of many outside my Manor. I was tolerated for my connections to the other daywalkers, but they, too, had become wary of me, believing me to be a turncoat.

I existed yet did not truly belong anywhere. But when I looked at Isolde, I felt like I had found my home.

"Isolde?" Liam was shaking me, rolling me off him and onto the bed. I shook off the remnants of the memory.

"You knew? About Will and Aurora? Why didn't you tell me?!" I demanded. Liam paused for a moment before answering.

"I didn't tell you because I didn't want to do anything that would sour your memories with Will. I know he did love you very much. As did Aurora."

I fought back the urge to take my anger out on him. I looked away from him for a moment and felt a strange sensation in my eyes. Almost like they flashed. Once I took a few deep breaths, I looked back at him again.

He watched me closely, and I nodded at him.

His response didn't make me feel even slightly better about the fact that my fiance and twin had been sneaking around behind my back, but I knew Liam wasn't responsible for either of their actions.

He kissed my forehead, and I allowed him to pull me close, drawing my back to his chest to spoon me. I forced myself to focus on those first traces of his feelings towards me that had stirred in that memory. The love that was buried beneath the protectiveness.

Sleep eventually claimed us both, but he kept his tight grip on me, even in slumber.

I awoke a few hours later, with Liam still asleep beside me, and finally allowed myself to remember the events of the last night of my human life. I recalled the moment when Liam's twin brother, Connor, had touched my forehead and unlocked memories that had been taken from me by the Order. I knew it had apparently been done for my own good, but the knowledge that my memories had been manipulated so that I would end up exactly how I was now... That wasn't okay with me. I was doing my best to ignore Liam's part in the web of lies, but I knew I would eventually have to ask him the tough questions. I had spent the past eight months doing everything I could to keep my family safe, only to discover that my sister becoming a nightwalker was all a part of the Order's end game. Their goal was for me to become a vampire, no matter that I didn't want that for myself, that I had begun to develop abilities without becoming the very thing I feared most.

I remembered the anger I felt when Connor had revealed the truth, the sudden loss of trust in the people I believed to be loyal to me, including Liam. The man with his arms around me had become my most trusted confidant in the past eight months, and in one moment, I learned that he may have been involved in keeping numerous secrets from me. About who I was and what I was apparently destined to become.

Although I loved him with all my heart, I struggled to accept that the lies had been for my own good. And my feelings towards the Order members who had been involved in this were doubly mixed, especially towards Patrice. The woman had become like a second mother to me, and to find out that not only had she known about the secrets and lies, but had been behind some of them... Let's just say I wasn't entirely sure if I was ready to face her yet.

My thoughts swirling in my head must have triggered something while another memory emerged.

"The prophecy must be wrong... Her powers were growing every day. I'm almost convinced she could take on Adam himself." I paced backwards and forwards in front of Patrice, where she sat behind her desk, shaking her head. I had been frantically attempting to get into Isolde's head ever since the team had called in that they had found the car that Isolde at her parent's house, along with Daniel, who was clinging to life while he gripped Celeste's body to him. I couldn't bring myself to mourn her death yet, the fear for Isolde overpowering everything else.

"The prophets have always held that her powers will be unbidden once she has become a vampire. But she must be the final twin to turn. It had to be after Aurora was finally turned, or it would have all been for nothing." I glared at Patrice, disgusted at the truths that had started to come out since Isolde left hours ago.

"The Order has been lying to her! Lying to me!" That my fate was tied to a prophecy I knew nothing about was just the latest occurrence to have me questioning everything I knew to be true about the Order.

"You knew there would be consequences when you started your relationship with her, Liam. You knew that there was an ultimate plan of the Order," Damon said from where he sat in the corner, and I fought the urge to throttle him. I had known this man for years but barely knew anything about him. Right now, I would happily beat him senseless.

"I didn't know anything about this, though! She is one of us! I can't accept that you were all sitting back, waiting for Aurora to be turned into a vampire before kicking this plan into motion!"

"If you do your part, Liam, she will be a daywalker like you. Then you can spend an eternity together once this war is won," Damon said with a smirk.

I couldn't believe he'd played that card. Patrice had the sense to look concerned when I continued to shoot murderous looks Damon's way.

"If I turn her, I doubt Isolde will ever want anything to do with me again. You know how the blood memories work. She will know everything, including all of the scheming the Order has been doing now. And that they sacrificed her and her twin sister to reach their ultimate goal." I couldn't stomach the idea of Isolde turning away from me.

"Well, who else would turn her, Liam? From what I understand, your contacts amongst the daywalkers are slowly drawing away from you. They don't trust you due to your connection to the Order," Patrice said, and I grimaced as I finally turned away from Damon to answer her.

"Eve would do it," I said.

Patrice raised an eyebrow.

"I highly doubt that the vampire who turned you would be the best one to turn Isolde. With the history between the pair of you? Doesn't Eve still hold out hope of you one day returning to her side? She turned you to become her lover, did she not?"

I felt uncomfortable having this conversation with Patrice. Few knew the truth behind my relationship with my sire, and I preferred not to think of it at the best times.

"If she knew the reasoning behind it, Eve would do it."

"I didn't realise you were still in contact with Eve. We need someone here now to do it." Patrice said, and I could hear her suspicions running through her thoughts.

"I don't know where Eve is now, but we can contact each other. If I needed her, she would come." That was a lie. I knew where Eve was. I knew Eve had always been nearby, keeping tabs on me. She generally left me alone, but I always knew she wasn't far.

"Have you told Isolde of Eve? How does she feel about her?"

I shifted uncomfortably, and Patrice didn't need me to respond.

"Ah, you haven't told her about your relationship with your sire. Tell me, Liam, what exactly do you and Isolde talk about, seeing that you haven't told her much about yourself?"

It was a question that Patrice didn't need me to answer.
She was well-practised at lying.
Especially to Isolde.

I lay silently for hours, stewing on the memory of the woman I had come to trust so much, just casually discussing my transition like it was nothing. When the darkness outside gave way to the first signs of dawn, Liam finally awoke, and I could feel his eyes on me without even looking at him.

"Hey... You OK?" He rubbed a hand over his face before propping himself up on his elbow to look down at me while I turned to face him.

"Not really... Life just became beyond screwed up, and I've been lying here for hours mulling it all over in my head."

He exhaled, taking my hand in his and running his thumb in circular motions over the back of it.

"Anything I can do to help?"

"Take me home?"

An hour later, I stood in front of my house and felt as though my stomach was in knots. I had fallen in love with this house the minute I first saw it, and part of its appeal had been its proximity to the river... The same river that now lapped around my ankles, and this was apparently after the water had receded... The dirty marks on the outside walls were above the windows, indicating that the entire house had been close to being completely underwater. While the house was close to the river, it had been slightly uphill, so the fact that there was still water at my ankles meant that other places further down the street were still completely covered. And no one had gotten any of my stuff out, which meant all my belongings had been under at least eight feet of dirty, disgusting river water.

This was just too poetic. My life was technically over, so why not have all of my worldly possessions completely destroyed. Yeah, it was all still there, but it was all completely ruined, exactly like me.

Looking around me, I could see that most of our neighbours had had the chance to get most of their valuables to safety, but not us.

Liam stood next to me. He had seen the news reports, so he'd had some idea of what to expect, but it was still a whole different experience seeing it in person. And it was harder when it was happening to someone you knew, or yourself, in my case.

"Couldn't anyone from the Order have come in and saved at least some of my stuff?" I asked.

Liam hesitated before responding.

"Well, I guess they were more concerned with your condition..."

Meaning they weren't sure that it was worth saving my stuff in case I woke up as a nightwalker.

"Good to see they are no longer playing at the whole 'family' thing. Seeing that I know the truth now and all." I couldn't hide the bitterness in my voice, and the look on Liam's face told me that my comment had hit home. Usually, the idea of hurting Liam would have upset me, but the thoughts I had been suppressing all night, mixed with the sight of my home, was enough to have all my emotions on overload once more.

"Isolde -" Liam started to speak, but I raised my hand to stop him.

"Not now, Liam. Not a good time to start with me." I walked towards the front door, the water rippling around my ankles, leaving Liam beside the four-wheel drive. I unlocked the front door with his key, but the wood of the door was swollen, making it difficult to open. I rammed my shoulder against the door, and it popped open with such force that I had to catch the door with my hand to keep from falling into the house. Another memory kicked in when my hand connected with the door handle, and I felt myself slipping away into someone else's mind once again.

"You're going to propose to Isolde?" I struggled to process the bomb that Will had just dropped on me, cunningly disguised as a happy announcement. Will hadn't been able to look me in the eye since Jacob and I had sat down. Around us, people were chatting away pleasantly, unaware that my heart was breaking. I had been waiting for this day for years and knew that was where Will and Isolde were headed, but having it confirmed still stung like a slap in the face.

"Yes. I thought it was time," Will said to Jacob from where he sat across from my boyfriend, preferring to look at Jacob instead. Though how that made him feel any less guilty was beyond me. I had trouble looking at Isolde these days, and lying in Jacob's arms at night was like a knife to the heart. I loved my boyfriend, but he wasn't Will Blake. And he never would be. I knew that Will was telling us

Before my turning, I had been developing psychic abilities and had visions triggered by touch. But the visions were usually linked to the location and the person, and that memory I'd just had from inside Aurora's mind had taken place before Will's death, before we'd ever entered this home.

"I just had a flash of one of Aurora's memories... When Will told her he was going to propose to me...." I was still staring into Liam's eyes, trying to understand everything.

"What? Aurora's memories? But... that's not possible..." Liam eyes drifted down to where my hand still gripped the door handle. I was surprised it hadn't exploded with the force I used to squeeze it. My knuckles had gone white.

"What is going on?" I asked.

Since I'd met him, Liam had always had the answer to everything. The look of utter confusion on his face while I looked to him for answers filled me with dread.

"I don't know... But, I know who might." Even before he said it, I knew what he would suggest and began shaking my head.

"We need to go and see the Order, Isolde."

"Absolutely not."

Chapter Five

UNFORTUNATELY, DEEP DOWN, I knew Liam was right, and that's how I found myself sitting in front of the manor about twenty minutes later, glaring at the rundown ruin that it was glamoured to look like from the outside. Liam sat silently in the driver's seat beside me, letting me take the lead on how this would play out. Although it had been his idea, I knew he had reservations about being here as well and would only walk through those doors when I asked him to. I tried to focus on that devotion rather than on his acts of deception. He'd been almost as much of a pawn in the Orders schemes as I was—emphasis on the word *almost*.

The fact that we had parked out the front instead of driving into the basement car park was proof enough that Liam had no intention of staying here any longer than necessary to get the answers we needed.

I took a deep breath, opened the passenger-side door, and stepped out, hearing Liam follow suit from the driver's side. I waited for him to join me on the curb. He took my hand, and we both stared at the house together.

"A week ago, this place was my haven. Now I can barely stomach the idea of walking inside and facing those people." I turned to look at Liam, who nodded. For him, the betrayal was almost worse. Yes, the secrets kept from me were harder to stomach, but Liam had lived amongst these people for centuries and had treated most of them like family. With the deaths of Katyana and now Celeste, along with the betrayal from Patrice, I'd lost the last of the people I'd grown closest to, but Liam had long relationships with almost all of them.

"How many of them know the truth?" I asked.

Liam glanced over at me and shrugged.

"I honestly don't know. I've only been discussing logistics with them for the past week. I haven't seen them since Eve and Ronson took us, and I've only spoken to Gerard." The fact that he hadn't spoken to Patrice spoke volumes about how much he intended to turn his back on them all.

Nodding at each other, we headed up the stairs and stepped inside. The entry foyer was empty, but Gerard came out from the training room a moment later and greeted us.

"I was wondering how long you two would stand out the front. Welcome back. I'm so glad you're okay." His genuine smile while he scanned me from head to toe gave me a sense that not everyone was involved in the deception. Liam studied him briefly before looking at me with a subtle nod. I assumed this meant that Gerard didn't appear to be keeping anything from us.

"Thanks, I guess...." I didn't bother to cover the coolness of my tone. I still didn't trust anyone in this building, and Gerard's eyebrows raised while he looked between myself and Liam. Liam shrugged at him.

"Where are Patrice and Damon?" I asked as I fixed my eyes on Gerard, who looked like he was about to step back. He swallowed and continued to look between Liam and me for a moment.

"What's going on?" Barbara entered the foyer from the dining room, followed by one of the newer transfers from Europe, Christian. They both stopped to survey the scene before them. Everyone was suddenly on edge. It was hard to miss the anger rolling off both of us, given that we were both ready to explode.

"I don't know..." Gerard looked over at her before turning back at us.

"I'll ask again. Where are Patrice and Damon?" I asked quietly, and Gerard stood up a little straighter, his features hardening.

"What's with the attitude?" Christian asked, and Barbara elbowed him, silencing him. Liam growled quietly beside me, and I looked over at him.

"They're in the command room."

I could tell Liam had gleaned this knowledge from one of their minds, and I nodded, leading the way. I heard the others rushing to follow us, not willing to stay back in case trouble was about to start.

Patrice turned from where she was standing in front of one of the many monitors, and her eyes widened when she took in my entrance. I felt Liam tense beside me in the fraction of a second before I was across the room, stopping immediately in front of Damon, who stood beside her. My face was so close to his that I could feel his sharp intake of breath before his eyes narrowed and glared into mine.

"You know..." Patrice had the sense to look extremely guilty from where she stood at his side, making no move to help him.

"That the Order sacrificed my sister for your ridiculous prophecy? Yeah, I fucking know." I returned my gaze to Damon, taking note of the flare of his nostrils and the glances he threw over my shoulder toward Gerard, Barbara and Christian. I glanced back at them briefly. I could tell from their faces that this was news to them. None of them had known about Aurora's part in the prophecy, it would seem. Whether they knew I was meant to become a vampire remained unknown. I looked back at Damon, allowing every drop of anger to show in my eyes. For his part, he didn't back down, instead choosing to meet my gaze head-on.

"Let me ask you. What wins wars? Who is considered to be on the side of good? Those who sacrifice the one for the good of many, or the ones who sacrifice the lives of all to save the one?"

I saw red, and before anyone could react, including Liam, I had Damon pinned to the wall, my hand at his throat, and his feet hanging in the air while I inspected him like the bug that he was.

"Save me the self-righteous bullshit." I tightened my grip on Damon's throat, and he gasped for air, his eyes wide while his legs kicked wildly beneath him. "The Order is broken. Have you all forgotten why we are called the Order of the Dragon in the first place? It's because, in all the legends, Dragons were protectors! Has it been so long since you all read why the original order members banded together in the first place?!" A moment passed before I let Damon go, and he sank to the floor before me when I stepped back. I watched with disgust while he rubbed his throat, desperately sucking down air. "I can't believe I followed along when you were so willing to throw innocents to the lions for slaughter."

"Isolde, it's not like that." Patrice looked like she would try to play down their deceit, but she clamped her mouth shut when Liam and I turned as one to glare at her.

"I have questions, and you will be answering them," I said. There would be no arguing from any of them. If they considered telling me more lies, Liam would know, and I would take them down. The look exchanged between Patrice and Damon indicated they were fully aware of this.

"What do you want to know?" Patrice asked, and I looked at Liam for a moment. Although we could no longer read each other's minds, it seemed we were still in sync when he gave me a slight nod.

"Firstly, Liam can no longer hear my thoughts, and I can't hear his anymore either. Why?"

Patrice hesitated for a moment before answering.

"That is something I am not sure of. From my understanding, Liam has always been able to hear everyone's thoughts, correct?" She looked over at Liam, and he nodded.

"Everyone except Adam, Connor and Eve, that is." I wasn't aware of that and looked at him with a raised eyebrow. He shook his head quickly, and I returned my gaze to Patrice. We would be discussing *that* bit of information later.

"Fine, next question. When we were at my house just now, I had a vision. A memory of Aurora's. It occurred when I touched our door handle, but the memory wasn't from the house; it occurred before Will's death. Do you have any idea why my abilities would now be changing?" There was another exchanged look between Damon and Patrice, and I narrowed my eyes, turning to look at Liam while he watched them closely.

"We don't know... This is all unknown now. Now that you've transitioned, we have no idea what you will be capable of. Only that you will be more powerful than all of us combined." Patrice answered me finally.

"You sent me off into a den of vipers, and you had no idea what would happen to me?" I asked, my words coming out with a growl. My patience was wearing dangerously thin, and Liam stepped closer. "Not the smartest thing to do when you all knew how important my family is to me and the fact that I was apparently going to be so powerful."

"We had no idea they would get to you before we had a chance to have someone turn you into a daywalker." Damon had the nerve to speak once more, and I looked down at him to see him shoot a look at Liam, making it obvious who the *someone* he was referring to was. He still hadn't moved from where he had slumped to the floor when I'd let go of him. At least he'd had some sense, I guess. However, speaking now was a big mistake.

"You could have told me the fucking truth before I went to save my parents." My voice continued to be low and dangerous, and Damon recoiled, wisely choosing to remain silent once again, seemingly aware that one more word from his mouth may lead, at the very least, to more pain. I continued staring at him, and Liam reached for my hand, squeezing my fingers, perhaps sensing that my emotions were so heightened that murder seemed like an excellent option.

"You knew what I was walking into. Maybe not everyone." I looked over at Gerard, Barbara and Christian. Gerard shook his head, his face showing his feelings about being left in the dark about the elders' plans. I looked back at Damon. "But you fucking knew. And you threw Aurora and me to the wolves." I turned and walked towards the door, stopping before I left and fixed a look back at them all. "I'm done being a fucking pawn in your little games. Before this is over, I will bring the Order to its knees." I sent Patrice a look filled with promise before turning and leaving the room, Liam close behind. I saw her shiver and relished it.

Fuck them all.

I entered my room upstairs and looked around, taking stock of what I had left there. Liam followed behind me and shut the door, sitting at my desk while I gathered everything together. There were a few dresses, some underwear and workout clothes. And my laptop. All that I had left.

Glancing over at Liam while I shoved the last of my clothes into a bag, I took in the look on his face—the wariness evident while he watched me move around the room.

"What is it?" I stopped before him, and he looked at my face, his eyes searching mine.

"I just don't know how to process all of this. Everything I knew to be true is a fucking lie…" Liam so seldom swore that I knew he must be reeling inside. I reached to touch his face, stroking his cheek.

"Welcome to my thought process for the last year," I said, and he held my gaze for a moment more before turning his head, kissing my palm, and standing up. He gathered me into his arms and squeezed me quickly before letting go and moving towards the door.

"I'm going to pack up my stuff. Stay here until I get back. The less we interact with everyone, the better, I think."

I nodded at him and took his place at my desk, turning on my laptop to check my messages. I had no idea where my phone had ended up, but my messages were linked to my computer, and I needed to get up to speed with the lies that the Order had been feeding my friends and family for the past week.

I scanned through the unanswered messages from several friends, surprised that anyone was still trying to reach out to me at this point. I had stepped away from so many people once the Order had come into my life. I felt a pang of regret at letting so many lifelong friendships fall to the side due to the Order and their lies. But I had felt safe here. Like I belonged.

I thought I had found a family.

Blinking back tears, I found the message trail between myself and Mum. Discussing the flood that impacted both our homes, the happenings with the family and her offers to have my sisters go to the house to get our stuff before the flood destroyed everything Aurora and I owned. When I saw that my response was that Liam and I were dealing with it, I growled. Not only had the Order fucked me over, but they had actively had my stuff destroyed. Rage boiled within me, along with the burning in my throat, and I wondered if Liam had been thinking of the others when he suggested we limit our interactions with them. I considered ignoring his advice, but then I saw a message from Mum that had come directly to my computer, not my phone, and I paused in my murderous thoughts to open it.

Mum:

Isolde, when you wake up, come and see me. We have things we need to discuss.

When I wake up? That seemed like an odd request.

The message had been sent this morning. I wondered why she'd sent the message to my computer rather than my phone.

I began tapping on the keyboard.

Me:

Mum?

The little message bubble immediately popped up, almost like she had been staring at her phone, waiting for me to respond.

Mum:

Where are you? Are you with the Order?

I gasped and stared at my computer in stunned silence.

Was this some sort of trick? Another message from an Order member, continuing to pull strings to manipulate me and my life? I grew even more wary when another bubble popped up.

Mum:

Isolde, if this is really you, you need to come and see me. Your father and I are staying with Breseis and Dean. As soon as you can get away, come here.

What did she mean by, 'if this is really you'? How did she know that there was a chance it wasn't me when she was messaging my phone?

I didn't know how to reply, and I was still staring at my computer when Liam came back into the room, a duffle bag slung over his shoulder. Seeing the look on my face, he came to stand beside me and looked down at the messages on my computer.

"What the hell?" His words were barely a whisper while I watched him read the messages.

"Does my mother know the truth?" I asked, and he looked at me with raised eyebrows, shaking his head.

"No... At least, not that I'm aware of. This has got to be some kind of trick... We need to be careful, Isolde. I have no idea who we can trust anymore." The concern on Liam's face was evident. I nodded, looking back at the messages before shutting my laptop and putting it into the bag filled with what was left of my belongings.

"Where to now?" I was unsure what to do next, and Liam took my hand, leading me out of my room. I paused briefly, giving it one last look, saying goodbye to the room that had become my haven. I doubted I would see it again. Liam squeezed my hand, and I looked up at him.

"We go home."

Chapter Six

HOME WAS A LARGE house, high on the hill in Ascot, overlooking the river and the city skyline beyond. I gaped at the beautiful home before us as Liam punched a code in on a panel at the gate.

"What is this place?" I asked, watching the gate slowly open in front of the car.

"My house," Liam said, looking over at me sheepishly.

"You have a house."

"I have a house."

"Since when do you have a house?!" I asked, and Liam chuckled as he drove towards a garage off the side of the large three-storey building.

"I bought it a few years ago. I needed somewhere to escape to when the house became too crowded. It all got too loud up here," he said, tapping the side of his head.

"Why didn't we ever come here?"

"Honestly, I rarely come here, even less so once we became involved. I didn't need to be alone as much once you came along." He smiled, and I felt myself melt a little at the sight of it.

"Does anyone else know about this place?" I asked. Liam pulled the car into the garage and pressed the button to close the automatic door behind us.

"No. This was the first place I ever bought for myself, and I just needed..." His words trailed off as we climbed out of the car.

"Something that was just yours?" I asked, looking at him over the bonnet of the car. He nodded with a small smile.

"Something that's ours, now."

I felt my chest tighten a little. *Ours.*

I let Liam lead the way inside from the garage and looked around in wonder. He watched me with a small smile as I took everything in while he gave me the tour.

Everything about this place reminded me of him. It was spacious, yet I noted the bookcases that lined the walls of almost every room except for the kitchen and several bathrooms—so many books. I could picture him sitting in any of the comfortable and mismatched armchairs spread through the house, book in hand, while he relaxed in the silence he so often craved.

The tour ended in the master bedroom that took up the entire third floor of the house. He dumped his bag in the walk-in wardrobe and came to take mine from me, dropping it next to his before returning to gather me in his arms. I breathed in his smell, allowing myself to appreciate this small moment of peace amongst all the chaos surrounding us. We hadn't spoken a word since we entered the room, and I was happy to stay silent a little longer.

"What do you need?" Liam whispered in my ear while he rubbed his hand up and down my back. His other hand rested against the back of my neck with his fingers tangled through my hair. I squeezed him tight, not yet ready to speak. I felt him nod before resting his chin on the top of my head. I appreciated him letting me sort through the mess in my mind. His soothing presence was a reminder of why I had fallen so hard for him, having always had the ability to provide me with an anchor amongst the raging storm around me. No matter what part he'd played in the Order's deception surrounding the truth about my future, he had always been there for me, his love unwavering.

After what could have been an eternity or mere minutes, I took a breath and stepped back to look up at him. The burning in my throat was quickly getting to a point where I could no longer ignore it, and something in my eyes must have given this away because he nodded and led me back down to the kitchen on the floor below.

"I arranged for some provisions to be delivered yesterday. I had no idea what would happen, but I had a feeling we'd end up here sometime in the next few days." He said, and I watched from a stool behind the bench while he returned to the garage again. I heard a fridge opening and closing before he returned carrying a large carton to the kitchen. Bringing it to the bench in front of me, he opened it, and I saw containers of blood inside.

"Who delivers cartons of animal blood?" I was intrigued about this side of his life that I had failed to ask about when I was alive, preferring to ignore that side of his world where possible. How naïve I had been.

"Daywalkers have contacts within the human world. A company arranges these sorts of things for us all over the world. The head of this company is a daywalker, but he does employ humans. They don't realise what the blood is used for, and he pays them well to ensure they don't ask questions."

I knew I had a lot to learn, but at this point, I was just grateful for the glass of blood that Liam had pressed into my hand. I drank it down and was relieved when the burning subsided. It was difficult to focus on anything else when my throat was on fire. When I'd finished, Liam took the glass from me and put it in the dishwasher. I watched while he finished his own glass of blood, the first I'd seen him have. He didn't seem to need it as often as I did. I hoped this meant that, eventually, the need for blood wouldn't be quite so overwhelming.

Our hunger sorted, I let Liam lead me into the lounge room and pull me down beside him on the couch. I snuggled into his side, and he wrapped an arm around me, holding me tightly to him. I let him draw comfort from me while he ran his fingers through the hair that fell down my back and side, something that he had often done over the past few months, and I'd come to take comfort from it myself.

After a few more moments of silence, he finally spoke the words I'd been avoiding thinking about.

"What do we do now?"

The fact that he was deferring to me concerned me. I had only been back for less than a day and had no answers to give.

"I honestly have no idea Liam. I need some time to sort through everything. To see what else is going to pop up in here." I tapped my temple, and he grimaced, understanding that I meant what other memories of his would surface.

He nodded and used his free hand to take mine, bringing it to his mouth to plant a kiss on the back of it, our fingers laced together.

"No matter what happens, what memories surface in there... I love you with all my heart, and I will be at your side," His voice was rough, and I sat back from his embrace to look him in the eye.

"I love you too. But we need to discuss some things, especially if I'm going to see things from your past that you might not want me to see."

Liam nodded after a moment, perhaps resigning himself to the inevitable and preparing himself for the truths he'd avoided for some time.

"Ask me anything. I won't keep anything from you anymore – you have my word," he said. I searched his face and saw the honesty there, the sadness that lay behind his eyes.

"How much of the truth about the Order did you know? About the prophecy? Or prophecies, as it turned out?" I allowed him to continue holding my hand whilst using the other hand to run his fingers through my hair. I sensed that what he would say would hurt and figured I'd let us both continue to draw comfort from those touches while he spoke.

"When I had that vision of you as a nightwalker, I spoke to Patrice. To ask her if that was a possibility. When she was answering me, a glimpse of the truth came through in her thoughts, and I questioned her on it. They had always told me that the prophecy was of a human who would have the power to end the war. I never questioned this, as when it was spoken about before me, no one's thoughts gave away any other versions of the prophecy. It seems as though certain members of the Order had become skilled at guarding their minds in a way I didn't know was possible. But Patrice slipped up. I found out the day after I first fed from you."

So he'd known for a few weeks and hadn't told me.

I felt my body tense up while I sorted through everything he had just said, and his grip on my hand tightened.

"I didn't tell you because I didn't want to believe it. And I only knew about the belief that you would become a vampire. I had no idea about the damn Gemini Prophecy." His voice shook at the mention of the prophecy that affected both of us. And our siblings alongside us. "If I'd known their plans for Aurora, I promise you, not only would I have told you, I would have been right by your side while you laid that place to ruins and told Aurora the truth."

I had felt that emotion when I'd seen his memory of talking to Patrice earlier and knew he was telling the truth. However, some of his other words prompted my next question.

"What other memories are you worried about? You told Patrice I would no longer want to be with you if I had your blood memories."

Liam searched my face for a moment before dropping my hand and getting up, going into the office that was off the room I currently sat in. I waited until he returned moments later, a book in hand. Judging by the worn leather binding, it was a very old book. I opened it up to see pages and pages of his handwriting.

"What's this?" I looked up at him. He stood before me with his arms hanging at his sides, his eyes downcast.

"One of my hundreds of journals. Start with this one. It will probably help trigger the memories. I have kept them all. They are in the study. I'll give you some space to go through them. Come and get me when you're ready." He dropped to his knees suddenly in front of me, knocking the book closed as he took my face in his hands and kissed my lips desperately, drawing my body into his and clinging to me. Almost as if he was attempting to give me something to hold onto before I stepped into the abyss.

Then he was gone, leaving me with the journal and the truths it and the others held.

I was suddenly wary of discovering things I'd rather not know. But I opened the book once more and began reading. Before long, I felt the now familiar sensation of being pulled into memory, and I closed my eyes, surrendering to the inevitable.

I slipped quietly from the bed I shared with Eve and pulled on my trousers. While I laced them up, I looked down at her sleeping form. In slumber, no one would ever know her true nature. Her mind was always one step ahead of everyone else, always thinking of some master plan. She claimed to love me, but it felt more like an obsession. Though deeply connected with her, I had no true love for her. Her memories had coursed through my veins while I lay dead. An eternity of memories now lay in my mind and my own of the last hundred and forty years. To know someone so wholly was something few could imagine. On a physical level, we worked exceptionally well together. But something was missing between us. I believed she'd lost the ability to feel love, and a millennia of walking amongst the human race had turned her heart cold. But I still yearned for what I once thought I didn't need. In life, I had believed that the love of a woman was unnecessary in my pursuit of the divine. After more than two lifetimes of experience, I knew that that wasn't so.

I stepped out into the cool night air, stepping around the drunk who had passed out in the doorway. If only he knew he'd chosen to fall asleep on the threshold of the home of vampires... The knowledge of our existence was still just as prevalent as it was one hundred and forty years ago, but I had left the backward thinking of the Estates long behind me. Eve had homes in many places throughout Europe, though we currently presided in her London base. I also kept a room with the Order in their Headquarters, but being around them too often made me miss my humanity, and I tended to become far too melancholy around them.

I walked past the Tower of London and couldn't help but marvel at its ability to send shivers down my spine. So much death had occurred there. I had only once been within its walls, at the beheading of Anne Boleyn. It had only been a few years after I had been turned. Eve had known Anne and her sister Mary before they became favourites of King Henry VIII and had watched with a morbid fascination while Anne rose far beyond her station in life to become Queen of England. But what goes up must come down. And she had fallen hard. I never knew if the accusations of witchcraft and adultery were true, but Eve had insisted on being there to witness her beheading. Having been close enough to have had some arterial blood splash on me after the axe fell, I felt her terror in the moments leading up to her death. I found my psychic connection with blood to be a rather heady experience. After that particular memory, I found it difficult to be near the Tower and its ominous presence. But it lay between myself and my destination, so on I went, ignoring the ghosts that I knew walked within its walls.

I continued down Eastcheap, finally reaching Pudding Lane. Like every night for the past month, a candle burned on the window ledge of the bakery. I smiled, feeling a warmth I'd now grown used to. After over a century of feeling nothing more than a vague interest in women, I believed that romantic love was only something from fairy tales. Now I knew that it had been because I had yet to meet the woman for whom all time stood still.

It had been three months ago when I first met her. I had been reading a book in a small park near where I now stood. It had been a warm afternoon, and I had looked up to see a young woman sitting on the bench beside me. She had some mending with her, and I could tell from her hands that she was working class, though she held herself like a woman far above her station in life. While I returned to reading Utopia, I found myself distracted when she began humming softly to herself whilst her hands worked away. Eventually giving up on the make-believe world of Sir Thomas More, I struck up a conversation with her. Intrigued by her intelligence, rare in a woman from the lower classes, I had lost myself in the conversation. Her name was Isabel, and she was a maid for the King's Baker, Thomas Farriner. She had lost her father and brother in the Great Plague, and her family had fallen below their station. As she was the only person able to support her mother and remaining siblings, she worked seven days a week, though Thomas gave her Sunday mornings off to attend Church. I had smiled at that, knowing she was meant to be at Church now.

"Oh, but it was just too nice a day to be cooped up in Church. God will forgive me just this once. And I had so much mending to do anyway."

She returned the following Sunday. And the next. I doubted she had set foot in that Church once since the passing of her father and brother, using those mornings off to have some time to herself instead. It was refreshing to meet someone who rebelled against the doctrines of the Church, yet at the same time, the small part of me that still remembered the need to spend Sundays communing with the Almighty thought she was being careless with her immortal soul. I knew my fate was to spend eternity roaming the Earth, never standing before the Gates of Heaven. But she shouldn't have to miss that.

I discussed many things with her - philosophy, art, and religion. Her father had been a scholar, responsible for her education, which was usually overlooked in daughters. Many a day, she had sat at her father's knee while he read to her from the writings of Aristotle and his contemporaries.

I had started to look forward to our Sunday morning discussions, and when the first Sunday came that she did not appear, I found myself seeking her out at the bakery that night. It was her job each evening to ensure the fires were put out, which meant she was the last one there every night. It was that night that I realised what my true feelings were for her. To discover that she, too, felt the same way was beyond comprehension. She had not come that morning, as she feared that her feelings for me were inappropriate and thought it best that she not see me. But when I found her alone that evening, our mutual attraction was something that the two of us could no longer deny.

The first kiss had been like nothing I'd ever experienced, alive or undead, and I knew she, too, felt the connection between us. I had returned every night since, and tonight was no exception.

Isabel was busy with the ovens in the back, and I let myself in, playing absently with the flower I had snatched from a nearby garden along the way.

"Liam, is that you?" Isabel entered the main room, and I smiled at the flour in her hair and all over her clothes. She was still the most beautiful woman I had ever met, even covered in flour. And I had met a lot of women. She had long auburn hair, beautiful green eyes, and a creamy, clear complexion.

She smiled coyly at me then, and I realised I had been staring at her. Wordlessly, I handed her the flower, and she kissed me softly. I pulled her close, kissing her hungrily. She kissed me back with the same fierceness, the kiss grow-ing deeper and hungrier. At that moment, I realised we were about to cross the invisible line we had drawn. We had never kissed like this before, with such abandon, and I wondered if I should stop this before things went too far.

Isabel never stopped, though. She was the sort of person who, once they made a decision, there was no turning back. When we shed our clothes, I was determined to make her first time as memorable as possible, pleasuring her in ways that had her coming apart in my hands and against my lips, eliciting moans she had no idea she was capable of. I revelled in the thoughts that cascaded through her mind while I brought her to orgasm as often as her body would allow.

Afterwards, when we lay beneath the window, our arms wrapped around each other, I wondered if I would ever feel this content again.

But I was only given that one brief moment to ponder this.

"Oh, my dear brother. How touching it is to see you with a woman finally. Aside from Eve, of course, though I don't think she counts." My head snapped up to see Connor lurking in the doorway.

Over the past century and a half, I had often crossed paths with Connor. Always the antagonist, Connor was prone to appear when I least expected it, catching me off guard and proving to me just how much of a monster he had become. I had witnessed the massacre of many people at the hands of himself and his followers and had fought against them so many times in this endless war between our two bloodlines.

I leapt to my feet, placing myself between Isabel and Connor. Isabel attempted to cover herself while Connor leered at her, looking her over with appreciation.

"I must say, Liam, you truly have impeccable taste," Connor said with a laugh, and I growled. Isabel pulled her dress back on and stood slightly behind me, getting her first good look at our intruder. She gasped, looking between us, seeing the identical features. Her thoughts were chaotic while she took in the predatory look in my brother's eyes and sensed that something wasn't right with him.

"Liam. What is going on? Who is this man?" She asked, her voice higher than usual, and Connor smirked.

"I'm hurt. Although, I'm not surprised that he has not mentioned his twin brother. He is so very ashamed of me."

"Liam?" Isabel repeated my name, her eyes still locked on my twin.

"Am I to understand, dear brother, that you haven't told your lover the truth of who you are?" Connor's eyes glinted in the moonlight, though the startling blue glowed, even without the help of light.

I glared at Connor, seeing Isabel swallow hard and begin to back away out of the corner of my eye.

"What are you?" I looked over at her and realised it wasn't my brother causing her to begin to flee, with her gaze now fixed on me.

"Isabel, don't be scared. I swear, you have nothing to fear from me."

She shook her head.

"No. Something is wrong here. Tell me what you are!" She demanded.

"Oh, this is fun! Go on, Liam. Tell her what we are." The sound of Connor laughing again set my teeth on edge.

"You and I are nothing alike, Connor. You are a creature of pure evil." I glowered at him.

"I doubt that will matter to your true love. A vampire is a vampire to the human race. They don't understand the difference. If there truly is any." Connor shrugged, and I wanted to punch him even more than usual.

"Vampire." I heard the word escape Isabel's lips, though she had barely whispered it. I heard the fear and realisation in that one word and saw it pass over her face. I felt my heart tighten as though someone gripped it tightly in their fist.

"Isabel, I can explain." I reached out to her, but she recoiled from me.

Like my touch would burn her.

"No, stay away from me!" The fear was written all over her face now, her eyes searching wildly for a means to escape. She ducked past me and ran up the stairs to the house above,

unknowingly fleeing to where I could not follow, having not been invited. Every crashing footfall on the stairs was like a knife thrust into my chest, and I struggled to contain the emotions running through me.

"Oh, dear. That didn't go so well." Connor's words brought me back to myself, and I turned on him in a blind rage. He didn't expect the fury of my attack and fell to the ground in surprise while I punched him with my fists mercilessly. I saw an expression cross his face that I couldn't place before he threw me off and jumped back to his feet, towering over me when I slumped against the wall, my rage giving away to despair.

"Why do you insist on ruining everything!" I wished the words had not escaped my lips, yet the sneer I expected did not come.

He stood, looking at me with the same expression I'd seen moments ago. Was that pity? Remorse? It wasn't possible. Nightwalkers weren't capable of such emotions. Whatever it had been, it was gone instantly, and I knew I must have imagined it.

"Life never goes according to plan, little brother. You should know that. I stopped her from making the biggest mistake of her life."

"Since when do you care about the lives of humans?" I asked, and Connor shrugged, not bothering to answer, before he turned and walked away.

After what felt like an eternity, I got to my feet again. I had been undressed throughout the entire exchange, and I struggled to put my clothes back on before fleeing into the night, wanting to put as much distance between myself and this place as possible.

I spent the next few hours stalking through the shadows, wavering between anger and despair. After a while, I realised that the night's noises were louder than usual, and I pushed myself out of the dark cloud I was in to realise that the noises I heard were not the typical sounds of the dark streets of London. I could hear voices raised in fear and people yelling—the sound of fire crackling. I looked back the way I had come and saw a bright glow in the distance. From where I stood on Tower Hill, I could see a great ball of fire. It spread from building to building at a speed I could not comprehend, and I realised that Isabel was right in the middle of it all. Fear, unlike anything I'd felt since the night my mother was murdered before my eyes, crashed over me, and I began running towards the flames. A crowd of people met me when I drew closer, fleeing from the path of the fire. The crowd was too strong, and I was swept away with them, unable to return. But I knew in my heart that it was too late. If what I was hearing was true, that the fire had begun at the bakery, then this was all my fault. Isabel was most likely dead, destroyed in the fire, when an unattended oven had set the bakery and surrounding buildings alight. I couldn't bear the agony that tore through my heart.

I felt the journal slipping from my fingers while I came out of the memory. The knowledge that Liam had somehow been responsible for the Great Fire of London rocketed in my head. With a shaky breath, I reached for the journal where it had fallen onto the floor, being pulled into another memory as my fingers brushed the cover.

But the memory was not one of Liam's.

Chapter Seven

I LOOKED DOWN AT *my brother's face while he slumped against the wall where I had just thrown him. I had taken every hit from his fists and willed myself to fight back, but I knew I deserved every blow he had rained down upon me. I followed his gaze to where he stared at the stairs that his lover had run up moments ago.*

I knew I was supposed to relish the agony I had caused him, but I felt only remorse. Every exchange between myself and Liam this past century and a half had been bittersweet. Seeing my once devout and sheltered brother step into the real world and experience things he would not have done if I hadn't made the choices I had gave me some joy. Still, knowing that he and I were destined to continue to walk for hundreds of years across this wretched planet, mortal enemies instead of allies, was a lot to stomach. Sometimes, I wondered at the decision I had made all those years ago. At the path I had chosen for us both. To begin a chain of painful yet necessary events. Or so that witch had said. I had often replayed the words whispered to me long ago on a night in an abandoned Church. Of a destiny that I was told belonged to me. To me and Liam. To two women yet to be born.

Moments like this made me wish to go back and make different choices. But of all my powers, the ability to change the past was not one of them.

I shook my head. The fog that had descended with the memory that didn't belong to Liam finally lifted, and I stared at the journal in my hand. How had I just seen Connor's memory? And what *was* that? It didn't seem like the sort of memory that belonged to a creature of pure evil like the one I had met—the one who had turned my twin sister against me and fed upon me with delight.

I sat on that couch for hours, surrounded by Liam's journals, immersing myself in his words. I tuned into the memories that each one triggered within me until I had trouble discerning where he ended, and I began.

There was still so much I didn't know, but I had seen enough for the night, and although I felt a deep resentment growing for Eve, I had yet to come across anything that made my feelings for Liam disappear. If anything, watching what he had been through, at how every potential relationship had been destroyed by either Eve or his brother, made me love him more. For his resilience in surviving the last five hundred years, watching members of the Order that he had grown close to grow old and die eventually. My heart broke knowing how alone he felt amongst the daywalkers due to his ties to the Order.

It was all a lot to take in. For him to have continued to be the man I had grown to love, to retain the ability to love so wholeheartedly and allow me into his heart... It wasn't anger that filled me now, only compassion and love.

I was sure I still had yet to see many things, but I craved his closeness now more than the need to learn more about his eternal life.

Rising from the couch, I went looking for the man who held my heart so tightly, finding him brooding while lying on the bed, staring at the ceiling. I came to stand by him, and the look on his face when he looked at me felt like someone had taken my heart in their hand and squeezed it so hard that it might explode. He was so convinced I would turn against him, believing himself to be unloveable because of several lifetimes of choices he had been forced to make.

I reached down and ran my fingers gently through his hair, and he closed his eyes, leaning into my touch.

"Look at me, Liam."

He opened his eyes and looked into mine, both of us able to see each other clearly despite the darkness that had fallen. One of the advantages of being a vampire was that I would no longer need to bother finding a light switch at night. He searched my face while I continued running my fingers through his hair.

I searched for the words to give him some comfort that my feelings hadn't changed.

"Nothing you have seen and done will change my love for you. I see you, Liam, and I do not turn away from everything you are."

He sighed quietly and shook his head.

"You have only been in there for a few hours. There is no possible way you could have seen every bad decision I've made. Every life I've ultimately been responsible for ending. All the people hurt either by me or because of me."

He truly believed that he was not worthy of my love.

I felt my heart break a little at the resignation behind his words and knew that nothing I said could change his mind. So I decided to show him in the only way I knew how.

I moved to lay on top of him, and although his expression didn't change, he reached around to hold me against him, anchoring my body to his. I placed my hand against his cheek, forcing him to continue looking me in the eye while my other hand returned to stroke his hair. I rested my forehead against his, and we both closed our eyes, taking comfort in the closeness. A sense of peace settled over me. The rest of the world ceased to exist, and it was just us.

"You are my world, Liam. Yes, I'm sure there are moments in your past that you aren't proud of. Choices that you have made that may hurt me. But what we have, what this is between us... It's the truest, most genuine feeling I've ever felt. I choose you, Liam, regardless of any ridiculous prophecy that has been uttered about us. Despite every heartache that we have both experienced. I choose you." I moved my hand from his cheek to touch his chest, covering the place where his heart was still beating by some miracle. Beating for me. "I choose this." With my heightened sense, I could hear his heart beating quickly, and I opened my eyes again, finding him looking at me. The love he felt for me shone through unshed tears. He released a shaky breath, and his lips met mine in a slow, tentative kiss. I deepened the kiss, and we continued like there were no outside pressures.

As though we had all the time in the world. Where earlier, our joining had been filled with need, this was to be slow and full of love.

He rolled me gently onto my back and began moving his lips down my body, reaching down to pull my top up. I sat up to remove it and unhooked my bra, watching him remove his shirt with one swift tug over his head.

His mouth returned to my collarbone, and he eased me back onto the bed, moving his lips slowly down to my right breast, sucking gently while I let out a whisper of a moan and ran my fingers through his hair. His eyes met mine while he ran his tongue over my nipple before moving to the other side and giving the other breast equal attention. I arched into his touch, and he chuckled, sending a shiver through me.

I wondered if I could come just from the attention he gave my breasts. He seemed intent on finding out while spending more time on my breasts than he had ever done before, and I was panting with need by the time he started moving down my body.

He moved between my legs, kneeling on the floor and pulling me gently towards the edge of the bed. He began undoing each button on the opening of my jeans before raising my hips so that he could slide them, along with my underwear, down my legs and leave me bare before him.

I raised myself onto my elbows to watch while he placed both my legs over his shoulders and lowered his mouth to the bundle of nerves between my legs. I gasped at the first contact, my head falling back when he began to work me up with his tongue.

It wasn't long before I was moaning in ecstasy as the first orgasm began rolling through me.

I met his mouth with my own when he stood up and bent over to kiss me from where I half sat up, the shock waves still running through me and causing me to shiver uncontrollably.

He moved his hand to continue where his lips had been only moments before, circling with his thumb and thrusting inside of me with two fingers. At the same time, his mouth returned to my breasts again, moving slowly from one to the other while I writhed beneath him, panting loudly and gasping as another orgasm built within me.

"Come undone, Isolde." His words vibrated against my breast while he continued circling it with his tongue, and I did just that, crying out when I came again. Slowly, the ringing in my ears and stars in my eyes cleared. I met his gaze while he looked down at me, his fingers still inside me to give me something to ride out the wave of ecstasy on.

"You're wearing too many clothes." I sat up and began undoing the fly on his jeans, and he shed them quickly. I ran my hand down his erection slowly and began pumping my hand up and down, intending to take him in my mouth. He shook his head, pushing me back onto the bed and helping me shimmy back up so that he lay on top of me, nudging my entrance when I wrapped my legs around him.

"I just need to be inside you now." He pushed slowly into me, and I arched my back to meet him. He moaned quietly when I used my internal muscles to squeeze gently, but he didn't move, instead stopping to look into my eyes. He lowered his lips to mine and kissed me softly with the first roll of his hips, and I felt my eyes roll back in my head at the feel of him inside of me. At the pleasure that bloomed with every, oh so slow thrust.

"Every part of me, Isolde. Everything. It's all yours." He whispered the words between the gentle kisses he moved down my throat between each thrust. I rolled my hips to meet each one, the two of us in sync.

It was like our souls had melded and become one. I knew every movement he would make before he made it, and my love for him grew stronger with each roll of our hips.

"I love you, Liam. You're mine." I claimed him with those words, and he slowly picked up the pace, almost like my words had broken the last wall within him.

I met him repeatedly until we came together with one final thrust, and our lips met again when we moaned in unison.

We stayed like that for the longest time, and I returned my hand to run my fingers through his hair again, our foreheads pressed together while we remained joined.

"Hold onto this moment, Liam. Keep it in your heart, like I will. This is real. This is us." I kissed his lips, feeling him nod while he kissed me back.

"I love you, Isolde." He pressed a kiss to my forehead before rolling off of me. We showered together in the large bathroom attached to the master bedroom before settling back on the bed together, foreheads touching, with our arms wrapped around each other and legs tangled together. As we fell asleep, I felt the now familiar sensation of slipping into a memory.

"So, you've awakened." Liam stood before me, and I looked around, unsure of where I was or what was happening.

"What do you mean? You've been with me all day."

His laugh was low, the sound familiar, yet not one I'd ever heard from the man I loved.

"Connor." I took a step away from him. He smirked at me before sketching a low bow.

"In the flesh... well, not really, as this is a dream. I believe in the present you are currently lying wrapped around that dear brother of mine, having both exhausted yourselves thoroughly after constantly comforting each other that your love is eternal, and so on." His words were meant to be scornful, and yet I sensed something else behind them. I ignored the curiosity I felt at him knowing what was happening in the real world, and instead studied him closely while he continued to watch me.

"You sound like you might be jealous, Connor." I raised an eyebrow.

"Hardly," he said with a scoff. Although he waved the words away, I could sense the truth and found that interesting. Everything I had come to understand about the man before me led me to the conclusion that nothing of the brother Liam had loved remained. And yet, there was something beneath the surface.

I could tell this interaction wasn't going as he thought it should, and he glowered at me for a moment. I felt my lips curl up, delighting in the knowledge that I had unsettled him in a way he wasn't expecting.

"What can I do for you, Connor?" I noticed that the room we were in was the one we'd been in when he and Aurora had fed on me. My eyes fell on the chair I had been tied to before breaking out of my constraints and then roamed to the wall they had backed me against when they'd fed on me together. I could tell that he had chosen this location to rattle me, and I wasn't going to allow him the satisfaction of

knowing he had succeeded. I returned my gaze to him while I moved to sit on the chair, spinning it to sit on it backwards, and I smirked at the look that skittered across his features before the mask of evil fell over his face again.

"Just thought I'd see if this connection was in place, as I'd planned. That my mind had connected with yours."

I raised an eyebrow when he crossed his arms and leaned back so his butt rested against the table behind him while he studied me. It was a move I had seen his brother do countless times, and I found it very unsettling that even after all this time, their movements and mannerisms were still so similar. And that I seemed to find him just as attractive as Liam.

"I'm not a nightwalker if that's what you were coming to see." I had no idea what he was doing, so I took a stab in the dark.

He just smirked back, continuing to run his gaze over me.

"Aren't you? It doesn't seem like you're entirely a daywalker, either. I can sense the difference in you that I think you've already started to notice. The hunger for blood is more pronounced for you than for Liam, isn't it? Your anger is just a little bit faster and stronger than his towards those who have kept so many things from you both. You enjoyed pinning that asshole to the wall earlier. Relished the rush of power you felt while you watched him gasp for air and knew you could end his life."

I stared at him, maintaining the mask on my face that gave an air of boredom, but inside, I was shaking.

His smirk grew, and his eyes flashed, no longer blue but the same brown I had noticed previously—one of the many confusing things about this man.

"We're done with this conversation." I got to my feet and willed myself to wake up. Connor chuckled, remaining where he stood and nodded.

"For now. Sweet dreams, Isolde. I'll be seeing you."

The dream around us faded, and I woke suddenly, briefly disorientated, before I burrowed closer to Liam's chest and allowed him to hold me tighter in his sleep. It was a long time before I could close my eyes again, unable to shake the truth of Connor's words and not liking what they meant.

Chapter Eight

"OK, WE NEED A plan." Liam stood before me in the kitchen the following day, leaning back against the kitchen bench in a stance that was eerily similar to the one his brother had used in the dream the night before.

"I honestly have no idea what we should do next. Our list of allies has rapidly shrunk to the two people in this room." I said, and Liam grunted in response, nodding.

"I don't trust Eve and Ronson, and I sure as fuck don't trust the Order. But I need to see my family and make sure they are safe from Aurora, at the very least. And get in touch with Ainslie because I don't want her involved with the Order in any way." I needed a drink. Everything was a mess. "I can still drink and eat, right? Something besides blood?"

Liam nodded towards what I assumed was a liquor cabinet. I strode over to open the doors and was pleased to see a wide array of alcohol.

"Bit early, isn't it?" He raised an eyebrow when I poured myself a shot of whiskey.

"It's required right now. I need something to take the edge off." I threw my head back with the glass at my lips, welcoming the burning in my throat from something other than a need for blood.

"OK, so the immediate plan," I said as I clinked the glass back down on the bench, staring at it while I tried to sort through my thoughts. "We go and see my Mum and Dad. After we work out what to say, that will lead to them never setting foot inside that house again so that there is no risk of Aurora getting to them." Thankfully, Aurora had never lived with any of my sisters outside of Mum and Dad's place, so they were all safe at home, at the very least...

"How about the truth?"

I whipped my head up to look at Liam. Since we had met, it had been all about keeping the world of vampires a secret.

"The need to keep vampires a secret is all from the Order. Daywalkers couldn't give a shit if humans knew about them. They go about their lives. The Order's mission has been to keep humans in the dark, to keep order and control the narrative. I've been doing a fair bit of thinking over the past week, and I'm done following the party line. If telling your family the truth is what it takes to keep them safe, then that's what we'll do."

"Thank you." I felt love for him swell inside, and I wrapped my arms around his waist.

"But, we may need to use some of the Orders resources, as much as I hate to admit it," he said, and I growled against his chest. He put his hands on both of my shoulders and squeezed. "I know, but they can make the issues with the house side disappear. They have connections everywhere, and although I am still incredibly angry with Patrice and especially Damon, we need them for some things."

I disagreed with this, but I knew I needed to defer to Liam when it came to this sort of thing. He'd had far more experience than I did, and honestly, I didn't want to be the one making the decisions right now. My mind was still a chaotic mess, and I wasn't ready to deal with the idea of saving the world when I still couldn't even get a handle on this constant need for blood. Liam stepped back and pulled out his phone, and I moved towards the fridge to pour myself a glass of blood from a pitcher.

Liam's eyes tracked my movements while he spoke to Gerard. I wondered if he was concerned about how much blood I seemed to need. I'd already had far more than he had in the past twenty-four hours, but I'd assumed it was because of my newbie vampire status.

What if it wasn't normal?

Connors' words from last night still rattled around in my mind, and I knew deep down that it hadn't been a dream. I was sure he had been talking to me through a psychic connection he'd put in place for us, and I found it deeply unsettling that an evil vampire mastermind had access to my mind whenever he felt like coming for a visit.

Liam ended the call with Gerard and went to grab the car keys.

"I'm going to go and meet Gerard and arrange things to get a plan in motion for your family."

I opened my mouth to protest.

"With minimal input from the Order." He added.

I grimaced before nodding.

"Hang tight here. I'll be gone an hour, tops. And then we can go and see your family."

"You don't want me around any Order members right now, do you?" Maybe I was being paranoid, but I was concerned about being left out of this part of the plan and thought it was strange that Liam was leaving me behind. He let out a breath, his shoulders dropping a little.

"Honestly, no. But not because I'm worried that you might lose it. You're vulnerable right now, and I don't want them getting any further into your head than they already are. Until you've run the gauntlet with all the blood memories going through your mind, it's safest we minimise any contact with them until you've got a handle on your emotions. The first few weeks after the change are like dealing with a mental illness. Some really high highs, and some really low lows." He came close and pulled me tightly against his chest, wrapping his arms around me. I pressed my face against his neck, breathing in his comforting, familiar scent, letting it centre me once again. I knew this would be a regular occurrence and wondered if I would end up allowing this to become a crutch. I relied on his presence to make me feel less of a mess, and I wasn't sure how to feel about that.

"OK. Be safe. Don't let them get inside your head either, alright? This has all been a lot for you as well," I said. Our eyes locked on one another, a slight smile on his lips.

"Don't worry about me, my love. Nothing will take me from your side. Especially not anything that the Order will throw at me." He left with a nod and an all-too-brief kiss, and I was left alone with my thoughts.

I found myself back on the couch, surrounded by Liam's journals. I figured I might as well get back to jogging those blood memories and speed the process up, if possible.

I opened the closest one and discovered it was more recent, from when I was born. I began reading and was soon transported to that time in Liam's life.

I rounded the corner and saw Alana pacing back and forth in the hall outside my room. She saw me walking towards her and immediately rushed to meet me before I could make it further than four steps. I could tell she had just found out what had happened, and heard the rage and sorrow swirling through her thoughts. I could generally shut those thoughts out, but it had been a long day, and I was exhausted.

"Is it true? Did they make a mistake with me?" Her words were frantic, her eyes wild, and I worried, not for the first time today, how she would handle the complete change in her treatment that was about to occur. To go from being the chosen one to being just like the rest of the Order...

"Unfortunately, it seems like it. The child was born two weeks ago in Australia. The seers have just sent word. It appears her presence had been cloaked somehow until now, so they couldn't sense her." I could feel a tightening in my chest as she pressed a hand to her mouth, her eyes shining with unshed tears.

"How could this be? Why were they so convinced that it was me if there was even a chance they could be wrong? Did no one consider how this would affect me?" The tears started falling, and I reached out to comfort her, but she stepped away. "No. I can't bear your pity. Not after you broke my

heart." She fled down the hall towards her room, and I silently cursed my stupidity again.

Five years ago, during a brief dalliance, I discovered that her feelings for me had developed into something far stronger than what I had felt for her and had been forced to end it. It had been nothing more than physical interaction for me, a way to scratch the itch. Although time had passed since then, she still held a place for me in her heart, and I knew I should never have let it happen. I should have sought out someone else instead of this vulnerable young woman whose entire self-worth had been tied to her status in the Order. Hell, I should have just gone and shared a bed with Eve. At least the complications with her didn't cause me any regrets because I cared little for her emotional well-being. She had Ronson for the relationship shit, as much as she wished she could have it with me.

I let myself into my room and sat on the bed before flopping back and staring at the ceiling.

A knock sounded at the door, and I groaned, getting back up to let Patrice in. The benefit of hearing others' thoughts was that no one could ever really sneak up on me, even if it made it near impossible for a moment's peace when I was in this house.

"I see that Alana knows the truth?" Patrice asked, her face pale, and I nodded. "Well, we'll have to deal with that as best we can. But, for now, we need to organise setting up the new headquarters in Australia. Damon is already on a plane and wants you down there ASAP." The joys of being the only daywalker amongst the Order meant that I was forever on protection detail. I had thought this part of my existence was over now that Alana was past her twenty-fifth birthday and had been learning the skills to protect herself.

But the birth of this child explained why her skills hadn't developed any differently from those of other members of the Order before her.

I nodded and took the paperwork she handed me, which included a one-way plane ticket from Los Angeles to Brisbane, Australia. I had to admit, I wouldn't miss the USA, but I wasn't sure if Australia would be much better. I missed Europe and wished, not for the first time, that I wasn't tied so strongly to this group that dictated my eternal life and movements. At least Australia was someplace new. I had been in this country for far longer than I'd expected, and we'd never needed to be in Australia before now, with minimal nightwalker activity. They preferred areas further North, where the nights were longer in winter. Or at least, they had before. In recent years, their movements had become far less predictable.

"You leave tomorrow. There is a photo of the family in that file and as much information as they could gather on short notice. They were completely off the radar. I have no idea how this slipped through the cracks." Patrice's mind was racing, something that very seldom happened, and I wondered at the fact that, for once, the Order seemed to have slipped up. I shouldn't have found that humorous, but watching them all scramble to appear as though this wasn't the biggest fuck up had certainly provided some entertainment today. Amongst the daywalkers, the Order was viewed as humans with a puffed-up sense of importance, but they could prove annoying, so they mostly just gave them a wide berth. Eve had often voiced her disgust at my ties to the group.

Thoughts of Eve made me realise I should tell her and Ronson of this latest development.

With another groan and a longing look at my bed, I left my room again and headed off into the night.

Arriving at the palatial mansion in Orange County, I let myself into Eve's home, having long passed the formality of knocking. She had always preferred large properties and kept an entourage, so there were multiple rooms that other daywalkers resided in occasionally. That daywalkers refused to acknowledge the similarities between this setup and the covens of the nightwalkers was always a sticking point with the Order. Sometimes, there were more similarities than differences between the two. But as long as the daywalkers avoided murdering humans, the Order begrudgingly left them be. If only they knew the truth, that humans would willingly be fed upon for both pleasure and the chance at immortal life. I had never bothered to discuss it in detail with the Order. The less they knew, the better.

"Liam." Ronson greeted me gruffly when he entered the foyer, and I nodded at him.

He was a man of few words and had long accepted my presence in Eve's life. His thoughts were always guarded around me, and I never knew how he felt about her preference for multiple lovers, but I assumed he also took others to bed. For my part, I didn't particularly care. My relationship with my sire had long been nothing more than physical. I was aware that she was unhappy that she had no control over me, but at least she accepted what little of myself I offered up to her without question. When you were a few thousand years old, your access to human emotions became limited. I sometimes wondered about my own emotions and if I would soon become detached as well.

"Where's Eve?" I didn't bother conversing, and Ronson waved his hand towards the room he'd just exited. I walked

past him and entered the library, stopping at the sight of Eve standing naked before me. Her long hair was out and a complete mess. Ronson must have been using it to anchor her in whatever interesting position they'd been in moments earlier. It wasn't the first I'd come across them having just had sex or even midway through the act, and I had become used to it. I knew it wouldn't be the last time, either. The two of them were known for their very voracious sex life.

"Liam. What good timing. I still have some pent-up energy I need to expel. Ronson was going to find someone to join us. Care to be our third?" She knew I would say no. I had only ever joined a few times initially, but I preferred the sole focus of my sexual partners, and she knew it. Our tumbles between the sheets were just the two of us and, for me at least, was purely about finding physical pleasure before I left again.

"I'll be leaving in a moment. I just came with news. It appears that Alana is not the one that the prophecy foretold of. Another child has been born who matches the description. I'm being sent to Australia now to begin watching over her."

Eve raised an eyebrow, amusement playing across her beautiful face.

"Of course the prophecy wasn't about Alana. I told you that when the Order became fixated on her for some unknown reason. But you were so convinced that they knew everything that I didn't bother telling you that the girl was still due to be born. We have known of her existence for two weeks." She waved a dismissive hand, and my frustration grew. She had told me that she believed the Order was wrong when we had become aware of Alana's existence. But Eve hadn't bothered to advise that she knew when that

child would be born, and I'd just brushed it off as Eve not wanting to believe that the Order knew something before she did. I should have known better.

"One day, Liam, you will finally realise that the Order isn't the all-knowing power they believe themselves to be. Knowledge is power, and there is so much that they don't know. I do love it when you have these little moments, though. You will turn your back on them and return to us one day. We are always nearby, waiting for that day." She smiled her little, aggravating smile. The one that both annoyed the absolute shit out of me and turned me on. Her smile grew when I shifted slightly.

"I suppose Ronson can wait a little longer for the next round." She moved to sit on the edge of the large desk and widened her legs for me. I considered her position for a moment before shaking my head. I knew it infuriated her when I didn't take what was offered, but she had long since learned not to bother chasing me. Sex occurred when I allowed it, which had become less often nowadays. Still, she would have been a far safer bedfellow than what I had allowed to happen with Alana.

"I'll see you in Australia, Eve." I knew without question that they would be following behind. I turned and left the room, passing Ronson as he headed back in, already undoing the fly of his pants, with Michael following behind. Michael looked at me for a moment, and I could hear his thoughts. He wondered at my constant refusal to submit to Eve, and I felt my lips curl into a knowing smirk.

"Because I know how much it pisses her off," I said, letting the door close loudly behind me. It felt good to have control over something in my immortal existence. Even if it was just denying an ancient vampire of a good fuck.

I came back to myself, hearing the door open when Liam returned. I allowed myself a moment to ponder what I had just witnessed. At the knowledge that Eve had been aware of my birth and that the Order wasn't the all-knowing organisation they so often claimed to be. Something told me there was still a lot more that I had yet to find out, and I wondered how long it would be before I sat down with Eve and had a very frank conversation. A part of me knew that, after what I had just witnessed, Liam would not like that much at all.

Chapter Nine

"HOW DID IT GO?" I found Liam in the kitchen after abandoning my position in the library. He tossed the car keys in a bowl on the bench and pulled my phone out of his pocket.

"Gerard is going to arrange that the insurance assessor that goes out is one with connections to the Order, and they will ensure that the house is a complete knockdown and rebuild." He handed my phone to me.

"So, the home all my sisters and I grew up in will be knocked down... That's going to be a lot to process for everyone." I could only imagine my sisters' reactions, let alone my parents. But I knew it was necessary. As long as that house remained standing, it was a liability to any occupants.

"It was either that or take your approach and burn it to the ground... I didn't think that would be the way to go... Knocking down and rebuilding seemed like the less traumatic choice." He poured himself a glass of blood, which he drank whilst getting a pot of coffee going.

Blood and coffee, the breakfast of champions.

"Fair." I wiggled my phone in my hand. "So, who had this? I've already seen the messages sent to people, and I've gotta admit, I'm not thrilled."

"Gerard handed it to me, but he didn't tell me who had been sending the messages. We didn't meet at the Manor. I think yesterday's exchange has been a bit of an eye-opening experience for a few people. Trust is a little thin on the ground over there right now. He just said he swiped it on his way out the door."

It was nice to hear that we weren't the only ones disillusioned with the Order of the Dragon and its heavy-handed tactics.

"I wonder if getting a whole new phone might be better... I don't trust that they aren't tracking us using our phones. The less they know about our movements now, the better," I said. Liam pulled his phone out and stared at it.

"You're probably right. We'll get that sorted before we go see your parents."

"Do you know where my car has ended up? Is it still in the parking garage?" I hadn't even thought about it until now, but Liam had been using one of the Orders cars, and I knew they were all fitted with trackers.

"No. I traded with Gerard. Yours is now here. I figured it was time to start cutting all the ties that bound us to them. But we should get yours checked out for trackers to be safe."

I heaved a sigh and flopped onto the stool nearest to him.

"I hate this. Having to worry about being tracked, avoiding the people I thought I could trust... This is what the rest of our lives will be like, right?"

Liam came to stand next to me and ran a hand up and down my back while I put my head on my arms on the bench.

"This is all new to me too. I've been working alongside the Order for close to five hundred years... It's going to be an adjustment."

I sat up to look at him while he stared into the distance.

"I guess Eve is going to be happy."

He stiffened slightly before answering. I could tell he was still adjusting to me knowing about Eve and the other daywalkers associated with her.

"I trust them about as much as the Order right now. Everyone has their agendas, and knowing they want something from us is concerning."

I still hadn't told him about my connection to Connor, knowing that would most likely be the news that sent him over the edge. I'd wait to see how those interactions played out before I dropped that bombshell.

My phone alerted me to an incoming message, and I pulled it out of my pocket.

Mum:
Isolde, we need to talk. Call me once you're safe.

I stared at the message before showing it to Liam.

"Something is going on, Liam. This message, on top of the ones from yesterday... It's like Mum knows something."

He studied the message, his expression unreadable.

"You're right. We should head over there. Maybe she is worried because she hasn't seen you in person...." His words trailed off, but I knew he believed that about as much as I did.

"How could she possibly know anything about the Order?"

He hesitated before shrugging.

"Honestly, I'm realising how little I knew about anything. I wish I had answers for you, Isolde, but at the moment, I'm the last to know in most cases, so it seems."

I could tell this was really worrying him, so I let it drop. His entire existence was in question, and I remembered that feeling all too well. Instead, I got to my feet and wrapped my arms around his waist. His arms came around me, and he sighed, holding me close and resting his chin on my head. We stayed like that for a long time.

After a brief detour for Liam to grab us a new phone each, he pulled my car up outside Briseis and Dean's house an hour later. He had never been here before, and I'd never lived here...

"How do we get inside if Briseis doesn't say the words 'Come in' when she answers the door?" I turned to ask Liam, and he smiled.

"You'd be surprised how often people say something to that effect when you're at their door."

I thought about it for a moment and realised he was right. The first time he had appeared at my window, I had automatically tried to ask him if he wanted to come in, but he'd cut me off.

We walked up the front path together, and Liam knocked while I shifted from one foot to the other. How would my family react to the news I was about to drop on them? On the drive over, we'd agreed that we would have to go with some version of the truth. There was no other way we could think of to keep everyone safe from Aurora.

Briseis came to the door and immediately gathered me in a big hug when she stepped outside. She was the sister closest in age to Aurora and me, and I was godmother to her youngest daughter. We had always been close, and I was glad she was the one I would tell first out of all my sisters.

"Come in, come in." She waved us both on through, and I exchanged a small smile with Liam.

We followed my sister into her large kitchen, where my parents sat at the bench, finishing their breakfast. Briseis was getting her kids set up with cartoons in the lounge room while they ate their breakfast, and I studied Mum's face while she looked at me closely. Dad got to his feet and pulled me tightly into one of his comforting Dad hugs. But it didn't feel comforting now. His scent was causing an overload on my senses, and I took a deep breath, torn between the knowledge that this was my father and the overpowering smell of blood threatening to consume me. Over his shoulder, Mum went rigid, staring into my eyes, her jaw clenching hard while she gripped her coffee cup tightly. A range of emotions crossed her features. Shock.

Wonder. Despair. When she finally settled on fear, my suspicions were confirmed, and I forced myself to step back from Dad's arms.

"You know." My tone was flat. It wasn't a question. It was a statement. I knew the truth without her having to utter a word.

Dad looked at me, confused, but I paid no attention. I had no interest in anything but the truth, which seemed to be something Mum possessed. I studied her closely, and she swallowed hard. Her eyes continued to bore into mine as though she hoped she was wrong and was trying to find any sign of my former self. She eventually took her eyes off me and turned to look at Dad, who didn't know who to look at. In a less tense moment, I would have likened him to watching a tennis match. His confusion was beginning to give way to annoyance at not knowing what was happening.

"Know what? What's going on?" Never having been one to take a back seat in any situation, Dad was unaccustomed to being in the dark.

"You might as well give it up, Mum." I had never spoken to Mum the way I was now. My disappointment in her was laced through every word. Besides Aurora, Mum had always been someone I could count on. Never before would I have believed that she kept a secret from me. That she could lie to me. To realise that she had been lying to me for a very long time hurt more than I could ever have imagined. But then again, Aurora had been in love with my fiance and lied to me for years, so maybe I was just naive in believing I could trust anyone in my family.

"Abigail? What is she talking about?" Dad's voice started getting louder, and Mum sighed before taking a deep breath.

Like she was preparing herself for battle.

"Yes. I know."

And there it was. Confirmation that there was no one left in the world that I could trust.

"You know what I am." I crossed my arms, though whether it was to protect myself or to keep my anger in check, I didn't know. I felt Liam step close behind me when Mum glanced at him over my shoulder. I had no doubt the expression that was most likely on his face was making her nervous, but I didn't particularly care.

"What you are?! Would someone please tell me what is going on?" Dad demanded. Honestly, I half expected him to stomp his foot in frustration.

"I know about the Order, yes." Mum continued to ignore him, her tear-rimmed eyes searching mine. A small part of me wanted to tell her it was okay. But nothing about this was okay.

"And the rest?" I wanted to believe that was all she knew, that she didn't know about the prophecy and what I had been destined to become. But I had seen the look in her eyes.

"I know you're a vampire." The words tumbled from her lips. I didn't know who was hurt most by her knowledge as the first tears escaped her eyes. For his part, Dad just stared at her. He turned his incredulous gaze to me, finally noting my changed eyes, his expression demanding answers.

"Has your mother lost her mind?"

So, I was right in assuming that Dad didn't know any of this. It was only Mum who had lied to me.

That didn't make me feel any better.

"How? How do you know about the Order? How do you know what I am?"

Mum hesitated to answer for the longest time.

"Your Grandfather. He was a seventh son of a seventh son."

I felt Liam's hand on my shoulder tighten, and now it was my turn to be silent. Of all the scenarios I had come up with, this was the last thing I had ever imagined.

I watched her deflate before me, having completely given up any attempt to hide the truth any longer. Surprisingly, Dad remained silent, along with myself and Liam, obviously deciding to hear Mum out before writing us both off as crazy.

"My father, when he died, was just shy of two hundred years old. He'd left the Order when he met my mother. Not something that was easily done, as I'm sure you know, Liam." She glanced at Liam over my shoulder before continuing. "When they had only daughters, he was so relieved. He hadn't wanted to bring a son into the same life he'd been forced to live."

I nodded, understanding why my grandfather wouldn't want to pass his curse on to the next generation.

Mum looked down at her hands while she shared this secret she'd kept for so long.

"I knew nothing about this until your father and I learned we were having a second set of twin girls. Seven daughters. Born to his seventh daughter. My father was beside himself. He'd worried when I married your father, not because he didn't like him, but because he was a seventh son." She said, and Dad's eyebrows flew up at this. "Of course, he'd told himself the chances of us having seven children were slim, let alone having seven daughters... He knew about the prophecy, you see..." She let out a ragged breath, barely keeping her emotions in check.

"So that's why Grandad always treated me differently to everyone else..." I had always known I was my grandfather's favourite among his many grandchildren. Now I knew it was because, out of all his offspring and their children, I was the one who would understand him the most. Mum watched me while I processed all of this.

"When he told me all of this, I swore he'd begun to lose his mind to old age. Vampires weren't real, and neither were prophecies. I didn't believe him, as he and my mother had kept the truth of his age and background a secret for my entire life."

"What changed your mind then?" In my desperate need to know the truth, all my questions came out as demands.

"Your change in character after you turned twenty-five. Your sudden fear of the dark and the way you jumped at shadows. And then Will's murder confirmed it all."

"Why didn't you say anything?!" It was the closest I had come to yelling since we entered the room, and I struggled to keep the desperate anger within from boiling over.

"Because I wasn't meant to know!" Mum yelled back, her eyes wide. "I know how the Order works. Your grandfather explained it all. I would have had my memory erased, possibly even lost you for good. They had the power to make us all forget that you ever existed, to believe that we had only six daughters instead of seven. And I couldn't risk that." Her voice was pleading, the tears flowing freely down her face.

"I still don't understand... You said Isolde is a vampire ..." Dad said quietly, staring at me.

"Because she is a vampire now," Mum whispered, almost choking on the words.

"Did you... Are you saying it was Isolde who murdered Will?! How could you believe such a thing?!"

She shook her head frantically.

"Of course not! No one who saw the grief she experienced would ever believe that Isolde had anything to do with how Will died."

"Then what are you saying?" Dad threw his hands up.

"You worked it out, didn't you? When you couldn't reach me..." I hadn't realised until that moment just how much Mum had known and how much she had kept from me. "Did you know they believed I had to become a vampire as part of the prophecy?! Did you know about Aurora?! Did you know what would happen to her?!"

She raised her hand to cover her mouth and shook her head vehemently while the words spewed out of me in anger, and Liam's grip tightened again.

"What do you mean? What about Aurora?" Tears had begun to well in her eyes, and I realised, with sickening clarity, that Mum had no idea what had happened to my sister. I felt Liam tense behind me.

"What are you talking about? What happened to Aurora?" Dad watched us closely while I tried to work out how to answer them both, and I steeled myself to drop the bombshell.

"She's a vampire."

"Like you?"

I shook my head slowly.

"I don't get it..."

Mum began to cry, and some of my anger dissipated.

"There are two different types of vampires. Daywalkers and nightwalkers. Nightwalkers are the creatures we hear about in horror movies and books. Creatures without any sense of right and wrong. Only the selfish need to meet their desires."

"And what's that?" There was a tone in Dad's voice now that I had never heard before. Fear.

"Their need for blood and power. And they kill without remorse to get it." Mum answered him this time, continuing to study me closely.

"And you're both telling me that Aurora is one of *them* now?"

I still wasn't sure if he believed everything we told him, so I nodded. He stared at me for a moment, the silence deafening.

"But... what does that make you?" He half whispered.

"Daywalkers are the opposite of nightwalkers. They are still immortal but maintain who they were before changing. They fight against the nightwalkers." Mum answered him again while he stared at me like I was a stranger.

"And that's what you are?" I could tell he was having trouble comprehending everything that had just been dropped on him, and I nodded slowly. I stared at my parents for a long time, wishing I could make them feel better.

I focussed on Mum. That she had started crying only at the mention of something happening to Aurora irked me, though I knew I was being slightly irrational.

"So, you only care that Aurora is a vampire? Am I ex-pendable? It was only me that you didn't care about." I said flatly.

"I care about you both! I didn't want anything to hap-pen to either of you! You were my babies. But I couldn't stop what happened to you. I was powerless. I never imag-ined that Aurora also had a role in this!"

"Did you know that it was foretold that I would be-come a vampire?! Did Grandad know that part of the prophecy?"

"No!" Mum's hands were clenched into fists at her sides.

At this moment, Briseis entered the room again and stopped short, taking in the sight of us all facing off in her kitchen.

"Okay... What did I miss?"

Chapter Ten

I SAT ON BRISEIS' back deck, staring out over the backyard. I'd left Liam inside with my family, unable to be around them any longer. Aside from the intense attack on my heightened vampire sense of smell, my anger and frustration consumed me.

Although Mum had told me that she knew, I was so tired of all the lies and feeling like everything I ever believed was bullshit. I'd heard the occasional raised voices from Dad and Briseis, and I was pretty sure more of my sisters had arrived, but still, I stayed where I was.

Liam came out to join me sometime later, and I heard people crying from inside. He sat on the top step beside me and put his arm around me. I automatically leaned into him to draw comfort from his presence once more.

"Are you ok?" He asked, tensing when I let out a low, humourless laugh.

"I don't know that I'll ever be ok again. Everything I've ever believed about myself, my family, the entire world...

It's all been complete bullshit." I stared down at my hands, willing the tears in my eyes to disappear.

"Do you want to come inside?"

I shook my head while I wiped away a tear that had escaped. He began running his hand up and down my back slowly.

"What's the point? I'm dead. They might as well grieve me like they are grieving Aurora."

Liam wrapped both arms around me then, and I buried my face into his chest, finally allowing myself to give in to all the rage and sorrow I felt.

We stayed there until nightfall, and Liam convinced me to return inside and face the rest of my family.

But when we got to our feet, a movement from the side of the house caught my eye. I exchanged a look with Liam, who nodded, indicating he'd seen it too. The hairs on the back of my neck raised, and I sensed the presence of a vampire in the dark.

At least that ability had remained.

We both moved silently. Liam handed me a spare stake, as I hadn't brought any. Liam took the lead while we moved as one, now able to work together without words after months of fighting side by side.

"Fancy meeting you here, Isolde."

The words came from the other side of the house, and we spun together. My heart began to race when Aurora stepped out of the shadows. A noise behind us had me looking back over my shoulder, and I saw Will approaching. Both their faces wore identical twisted grins.

"Leave. Now." I stared my sister down, but she just laughed.

"Why should I? You're here. Aren't you just as danger-ous to our family as I am?" She was surveying me slowly before meeting my gaze.

"You failed Aurora. Sorry to burst your bubble, but your attempt to turn me failed. I'm nothing like you."

She grinned again, opening her mouth to respond, but a sound from up on the deck made her pause, and we both looked up. My blood ran cold at the sight of two of our older sisters stepping out the door.

"Isolde? Are you out here?"

The feral look on Aurora's face unleashed something in me when Guinevere and Selena looked out over the railing and spotted us. They froze in place, and I moved quicker than they would have known possible, blocking Aurora's access to the stairs before she could reach them.

Will and Liam had begun fighting, but I focussed on my twin while I screamed for my sisters to get back in-side. Neither moved, and I groaned when even more of my family joined them instead, alerted by their screams once they'd noticed Will and Aurora. Exasperation and terror mingled inside me while I watched Aurora to see what she'd try to do next. They'd just learned about the presence of vampires, and now they were all hanging out in the dark, watching us fight. If we all survived this, I would do some severe telling-off.

"So, I see they all know?" Aurora said, waving a hand casually towards our family, completely ignoring the fight between Liam and Will right behind her.

"Yes. I thought it best that they know the truth."

Aurora laughed again.

"The truth?! You've been lying to everyone for a year, and now you're all up on your high horse about telling the truth? You're so full of shit, Isolde! Always having to be the good twin. Always the favourite. Well, too bad for you. They all know that's not true anymore." Aurora moved towards me with super speed and attempted to throw me aside. Although she had vampire strength and speed on her side, I had been trained to fight even before my change, and I blocked her fist before bringing my own up into her ribs. She flew back with a grunt, and I heard gasps behind me when she landed in the middle of the yard. I spun to face my family.

"Get. In. Side." I knew my tone was terrifying, which seemed to spur Mum into action. She and Dad began grabbing my sisters and dragging them back into the house. Thankfully, they went without a fuss, and I could return my attention to the scene before me. Undoubtedly, they were all pressed against any windows that overlooked this part of the yard. As long as they were inside, I didn't care.

Liam had also managed to knock Will across the yard and came to join me. We stood side by side, having shifted as one into position, ready for the next attack. Aurora and Will faced off against us when a shrill whistle sounded, and Liam's gaze snapped up to discern where it had come from. Aurora and Will immediately began moving back before turning and disappearing in a flash, leaving us staring after them.

I didn't dare take my eyes off where they had disappeared into the dark, but Liam continued to survey the trees and surrounding fence line. Slowly, the presence I had sensed disappeared, and I allowed myself to relax a bit.

"Any idea who called them off?" I still surveyed the area but saw Liam shake his head out of the corner of my eye.

"No, but my bets are on either Connor or Adam. I'd assume those two wouldn't be far when it comes to Will and Aurora. Especially not if they are tracking us."

I nodded while we backed up towards the stairs before quickly entering the house.

As soon as I closed the door, I was met with hysterical questions from my family.

"I thought you said Aurora was dead?!" Guinevere turned on Liam immediately, and I looked at Mum.

"Didn't you tell them the truth?"

She shook her head.

"No, I did tell them the truth, but Guinevere and Selena refused to believe me. However, I'm guessing that display outside has assisted in my attempts." She eyed my sisters, who at least had the decency to look chastened.

Aphrodite was standing to the side, her gaze roaming over me slowly.

"Does that mean what Mum said about you and Liam is also true?" She sounded scared, and I couldn't blame her, not with what she had just seen. Even without the 'Aurora's back from the dead' act, Will's presence had thrown them all into a chaotic mess.

"Well, I'm not sure what Mum said about Liam, but yes... I am a vampire now," I said, and Selena and Dido visibly recoiled from me. For her part, Briseis remained close, and I was relieved.

"But you're not like them, right?" Guinevere was still eyeing Liam up and down, seeming to hold him responsible for everything, judging by the angry look on her face. Unmoving, Liam just held her gaze. My sister had the sense to look away first.

"No. Liam and I aren't like Aurora and Will. We can walk in daylight, which Briseis, Mum, and Dad have already witnessed. And we don't feed on humans." I figured I'd leave out the part where we *could*. We just didn't *need* to.

"But... Aurora's... She's like the ones on TV..." Aphrodite's voice was so quiet, and her lower lip trembled. It broke my heart to witness my sisters trying to process this all. I nodded.

"Nothing of the Aurora that you all knew and loved remains," Liam answered from behind me, his chest to my back, and I leaned back into him.

"You all need to be wary now. Her coming here tonight proves that she isn't going to leave anyone alone. Please promise me, no matter what, you won't let her in your homes." I begged my sisters, and they all nodded, each processing their grief. I turned to look at Liam.

"We need to get the Order to put cloaking spells on everyone's homes. It's the only way we can at least guarantee everyone's safety when they are at home."

The fear for my family struck me then. Until now, my focus has been on how to talk to my family about Aurora's death. The enormity of what was ahead of me was starting to hit home.

"You all need to come up with a plan moving forward. I don't think I can protect you all at once, and I don't trust the Order to do it anymore, either." I looked at Mum again. "This falls on you now. You couldn't protect me, but you will damn well keep everyone else safe."

I was painfully aware of the tears reappearing in Mum's eyes. Dad looked like he wanted to say something in her defence, but he could see that I was also breaking apart.

"Liam and I will stay here tonight. It's unsafe for you to leave until we can get your houses cloaked. Call anyone you need to and tell them anything to ensure they don't leave the house if they hear anything outside. No matter what they hear." I looked at each of my sisters individually, and slowly, they all started to grasp the enormity of the situation and that their lives were all changed forever.

When everyone began talking at once, I became painfully aware that I was standing in a room full of humans. As my sisters closed in around me, every heartbeat grew louder until it was all I could hear, and the sweet smell of their blood began to wash over me.

I turned and left the room, needing to put myself as far from everyone and their grief as possible. It was all too much, and I was barely keeping it together.

Chapter Eleven

SOMETIME AFTER MIDNIGHT, WHILE I sat on the bench seat in the front room, looking out at the street for any movement, I heard Mum talking to Liam in the kitchen. My family had slowly moved to various rooms to get some sleep, having spoken to their significant others and attempted to ensure their safety. A few of my sisters had tried to leave to ensure their children and partners were safe, but I had again fought them to stay here. Liam had called Gerard, and it was only on the assurance that the Order would send someone to each house that I could convince them to stay.

"Was it you that turned Isolde?" Mum asked Liam.

"I tried to get to Isolde, to save her, but Aurora and my brother had already begun to feed on her... My only choice was that they turn her, and I had to kill her or attempt to turn her into a daywalker. It was something I hoped I'd never have to do." His voice was low, though he knew I could hear him, and I closed my eyes against the latest wave of grief. Silence fell over the kitchen for a few moments, and then Dad spoke up, doing nothing to keep quiet.

"You should have done a better job of protecting her."

"I know. There isn't a single part of me that doesn't feel responsible for what has happened."

I could picture Liam looking at Dad, wishing he had been able to protect his daughter instead of aiding in her descent into the paranormal.

"You said you had no idea about the prophecy about the twins... Did you know about the prophecy about Isolde becoming a vampire?" Mum asked softly.

"No, Abigail. I swear it to you. I had been told that she would be more powerful than anyone could imagine and that she would be responsible for ending this war. It wasn't until after Aurora took her that the elders finally let it slip in front of me. I don't even know how they managed to keep it from me all these years, which has weighed heavily on me."

I heard Mum sigh.

"My father spoke of the Order with fear and anger. He said the elders had kept many things from them, and he'd lost faith in their cause. He feared what they had planned for Isolde but told me that I couldn't do anything to stop them, or we'd lose her to them entirely. I wonder now if we could have hidden her away somewhere instead."

I could tell she was blaming herself, but I knew there was no way of hiding from the Order, not for a regular person. I stared down at the inside of my right wrist, idly tracing the golden tattoo. My thoughts wandered for a moment while I pondered, not for the first time, about its meaning and why my tattoo differed from all the other order members. I was tired of not knowing the answers to what lay before me.

"You couldn't have done that, Abigail. They have eyes everywhere." Liam said, echoing my thoughts. Mum began to cry. I assumed Dad was attempting to comfort her and wasn't surprised when Liam joined me a moment later, leaving them to their grief.

I looked up when he stopped beside me.

"We need to go and see the Order tomorrow. I want answers," I said while he gazed at me, and his jaw clenched. "Particularly, how they managed to keep all this shit from you for centuries when you can read minds."

It had been bugging me since I'd learned the truth, and I knew it was also plaguing him.

"In the morning, we'll go there first thing." He nodded, and we turned our gazes to the street, lost in our thoughts. I exhaled, feeling myself start to slip into another memory.

I finished checking into my hotel and dumped my suitcase in my room before heading off to find food, enjoying being alone for a change. The past few months had been awful, between losing Will and watching Isolde disappear, becoming involved with someone else so quickly. There was just something about Liam. I couldn't put my finger on it, but there seemed to be so much more that he knew than he was letting on. I still suspected Isolde and Liam were involved before Will's death. But maybe that was just my guilty conscience.

I bought myself some sushi and a drink, carrying it while I searched for somewhere comfortable to sit in the Botanical Gardens, overlooking the Opera House and Harbour Bridge. I'd always liked Sydney and had found myself toy-

ing with the idea of moving here lately. This conference was a chance to show work my capabilities, and network with the Sydney office and see if a transfer was possible. I didn't know how Jacob would feel about it, but I'd been feeling us drifting apart recently, and I knew that was my fault. Will's death had hit me hard, and I think Jacob had come to suspect the truth. We'd been spending less time together. Maybe a break was what we needed.

I stayed there until the sun was low on the horizon, admiring the sunset behind the bridge and reflecting off the curves of the Opera House. I knew the gardens were due to close and hustled to head back to my hotel before it grew too dark. I wasn't keen to be in the gardens in the dark on my own.

My hotel wasn't far, and I stopped to grab some food for breakfast in the morning. I needed a good night's sleep, and I'd be ready to take on the next week of work ahead of me. I'd worry about my personal life when I got back to Brisbane. I knew I needed to talk to my sister and attempt to fix the fracturing relationship, but I had no idea how to go about that when I still held so much resentment towards her. Most of it wasn't her fault - she had no idea about Will and me, but I was so angry at how easily she had moved on. Even though Liam was hot (even I could see that, no matter how much I didn't trust him), nothing explained how easily she had fallen for him and seemingly left behind all memories of Will.

I was so lost in thought that it took me a moment to notice that my hotel room door was open slightly. I stared at it, my heart racing, unsure whether I should go in or not. I was positive that the door had been locked when I left. I stayed in the hall for a few heartbeats more, but I heard no noise from inside, and I decided that whoever had broken in had already left. With a shaking hand, I pushed the door slowly open, looking around from the hallway. There was no movement, so I eased my way in slowly, wishing I had some sort of weapon with me.

My room was a mess, furniture strewn all over. My suitcase, whilst still closed, had been thrown into a corner and was sitting against the wall. But the stranger slumped in the corner was the most startling thing in the room. He didn't move, and I muffled a scream as I took in the way his head hung at an odd angle. As if it was broken. His eyes were open, and I could tell he was dead when I moved closer.

While I was staring at him, I heard a noise behind me, and I spun around, my heart racing so fast that all I could hear was it pounding in my ears.

The person standing before me couldn't possibly be here. Couldn't possibly be walking around. I backed up against the wall, avoiding the man at my feet.

"Will…" I barely whispered his name and felt the terror grow when he smiled at me, a cruel, twisted smile that I had never seen on his face before. With his new, startling blue eyes and how he carried himself, I sensed that this new version of Will was a skilled predator.

"Hi, Aurora. Have you missed me?"

I had no words. I wasn't even sure that I could speak through the terror. Will stepped aside while another two men came into the room with him. I did a double take when I recognised one of them as Liam.

"What… Liam…" I couldn't complete a coherent sentence, and I looked around the room wildly, searching in vain for some way around them all and out of this god-forsaken hotel room.

"Wrong. I'm the better-looking one." The man who wasn't Liam smiled almost sadly at me while he stood back behind Will and the third man.

"Twin... Liam never said he was a twin...."

Not that we'd ever spoken much, I'd mostly avoided getting to know him... I was starting to regret that now.

"Liam wouldn't have many nice things to say about me. He likes to pretend I don't exist. Easier that way." Not Liam said, and Will growled. *"Calm down, William. You'll get your shot at him soon enough."*

I stared at them, trying to deal with the fact that I was seeing them side by side. Even if he wasn't Liam, he looked exactly like his brother, and seeing him standing next to Will was unnerving.

I was so focused on the two of them that I hadn't noticed that the third man had moved closer until he stood before me. I could feel myself shaking uncontrollably while I stared into his cold, ice-blue eyes. Eyes that were the same as Will's. The same as Liam and his brother.

"Good girl, Aurora. Don't fight it... This is only going to hurt a little bit." The stranger pinned my shoulders against the wall while he whispered into my ear, and I felt tears start rolling down my face while he trailed his nose down my throat. I cried out when I felt a sudden, sharp pain where his teeth pierced the skin of my neck, and the last thing I saw was Will's gleeful smile and the sad, resigned expression on the face of Liam's twin. And then everything went black.

Chapter Twelve

I CAME OUT OF the memory and found myself in a ball, rocking back and forth, with tears rolling down my face. Liam was hovering over me, and my parents were behind him, with no idea what was happening. I struggled to gather myself, unable to look at any of them.

"Isolde? Baby, are you ok?" Mum moved tentatively towards me, but Liam flung an arm before her. He crouched before me to look at my eyes, searching my face. Although I couldn't read his thoughts, I could tell he was trying to work out what I'd seen of his memories, and I shook my head subtly.

"In the first weeks after turning, a vampire is exposed to the memories of the vampire who turned them. They already had them go through their minds while they were unconscious. That's what determines their temperament before they wake... But they relive the memories as if they are their own for weeks. In my case, because of how old my sire was, it went on for months. I'm not sure how long it will last for Isolde." Liam explained to my parents, although he never took his eyes off my face, watching while I brought myself back together.

"So, Isolde just experienced one of your memories?" Dad asked. I could tell that he was still unsure how to deal with the idea of speaking to the man who had turned his little girl into a vampire.

I took a deep breath and looked up at my parents, tearing my gaze from Liam's face. I had no idea how to explain that I had just witnessed my sister being turned into a nightwalker. Something I shouldn't be able to see as a daywalker.

"Yes," I said. I hated myself for lying, but something was happening inside me, and I wasn't ready to try and face it.

In the early morning hours, my parents finally retired to the room they had been staying in. We had spoken a little more after my episode, but I hadn't been able to tell them much, and we'd settled for trying to make a plan.

The hardest part had been finding where to go from here. We wanted to mourn the Aurora we knew, the daughter and sister that she had been. But we also couldn't tell people she had died. The genuine fear that she may show up at the homes of loved ones kept us from that reality. All we could agree on was that we needed to tell people that she was dangerous and to keep their distance. At this point, I needed to leave that with my family to deal with. I had too many other burdens to carry on my shoulders right now.

Liam had remained with me, neither of us having needed to sleep, and we watched the sun rise over the houses in the street.

"I spoke to Gerard. We should head to the manor soon. Get this conversation over with." I nodded, leaning into his side from where he sat with his arm around me.

We waited until some of my sisters came downstairs and told them we would inform them once their homes were safe before leaving.

While we drove back to the Manor, I stared out the window, trying to process everything that had happened in the last twenty-four hours.

"You doing okay over there?" Liam asked, pulling me from my musings when he turned the car into a service station.

"Not even remotely. Why are we here?"

He pointed at the fuel light.

"This just came on. I'll be five minutes, at most." He unbuckled his seatbelt and stepped out of the car. I stayed in the car for a moment before doing the same, and he looked at me in surprise over the roof.

"I can go pay." He raised an eyebrow at me and looked like he wanted to protest, but I didn't allow him to speak, turning to head inside. Once I stepped into the cool air conditioning, I was overwhelmed by the bright lights and smells. Too late, I remembered this was the first time I'd been somewhere public since I'd transitioned, and I understood why Liam had hesitated when I got out of the car when everything hit me all at once. The phone behind the glass partition at the counter rang, and it sounded like the volume was up to a hundred. The music on the radio screeched at me, the scent of body odour was making me nauseous, and all the bright lights and colourful items on the shelves made me feel like I needed to curl in a ball with my hands clamped over my ears. I must have looked like a crazy person while I stood frozen at the door, and the attendant at the counter ran her eyes over me. I forced myself to move.

I moved closer to the counter, and the smell from the attendant threatened to overpower me. Amongst all the other noise, I could hear the steady beat of her heart... And a gushing noise that I couldn't place.

With every step, the burning in my throat grew stronger again, and I realised, startlingly, that it was blood I was smelling. Her blood. And it was alluring and intoxicating. I wanted to wrap myself in it.

My gaze drifted to her throat, at the throbbing pulse in her neck, and I finally placed the gushing sound. It was her blood pumping beneath her skin.

I stopped a few steps away from the counter, fearing that if I were to move any closer, the need to leap over the counter and sink my teeth into the sweet spot where her shoulder met her neck would overpower everything else.

"Are you okay?" Her voice wavered a little. The woman looked about forty. She probably thought I was high. It would have been my first thought in her situation.

"Isolde. I've got it." Liam came up behind me, startling me. I'd been so fixated on the woman that I hadn't heard him enter the store. I stayed where I was while Liam paid for the fuel. He returned to me and gently took my hand, unfurling it from the fist that had formed at my side. He pulled me close to him and pressed his lips to my temple, guiding me from the store and back into the morning light.

The burning in my throat eased a fraction, and I allowed myself to relax into his side.

"Just breathe. I should have stopped you from going inside. That would have been too many senses triggered at once. We need to ease you into situations where you're exposed like that." He steered me towards the passenger door, and I slid into my seat. I looked down at my hands and saw that they were shaking from the effort of trying not to tear that poor woman's throat out. I waited until Liam had joined me in the car interior before speaking.

"I just... I wasn't expecting to be a threat to people..."

Liam paused in the motion of putting on his seat belt and shot me a confused look.

"What do you mean? I didn't think you were a threat to her. Did you think that was what I was worried about?"

I studied his face closely, unsure of how to respond.

"I just... All I could focus on was her blood..."

Liam continued to look at me with a furrowed brow.

"You mean the sound of her heart beating and the blood pumping?"

"Yeah..."

"Eventually, you'll get used to it. But you're not a threat to humans, Isolde. Daywalkers don't have the instincts that nightwalkers have. I'm not worried about that with you. I didn't want you to become overwhelmed with all of these changes right now, that's all. Let's ease into the outside world bit by bit, okay?"

I nodded absently. Perhaps he had been a vampire for so long that he no longer focused on the smell, the irresistible scent that had me ready to leap over that counter to get a small taste. Liam reached across the centre console and squeezed my hand.

"Let's go and get this over with." He turned the car on, and I watched the store slip away outside the car, wondering what had just happened. And whether I was indeed as safe as Liam believed I was.

Chapter Thirteen

TEN MINUTES LATER, WE stood in front of the manor again, and I struggled to keep my anger in check. I didn't want to talk to Patrice and especially didn't want anything to do with Damon, but we had too many questions that needed answers. Unfortunately, they were the ones who would be able to provide them.

Gerard was the first person we encountered again, having been waiting for us. He alerted Barbara, and she joined us while we headed into the conference room. Patrice was sitting at the table waiting for us. Gerard must have given her a heads up we were coming. I was glad that Damon seemed to have the sense to stay away. However, his cowardice, leaving Patrice alone to deal with the mess, further cemented my disgust with him.

"Gerard told me you had a run-in with Aurora and Will last night."

I raised an eyebrow at having our interaction with my dead sister and fiance be called a run-in.

"Yes," Liam stated, and we both remained standing whilst the others all took seats at the table. Other Order members came into the room and took seats as well, and I started to get an uneasy feeling. It looked like a full meeting had been called. I froze when Daniel entered the room, noting the wound and the bandage around his throat. I could feel the anger simmering off of him, though if it was directed towards me or the elders, I wasn't sure. I turned back to Patrice, unable to deal with Celeste's death yet.

"And Gerard also tells me that you have requested that the Order cloak the homes of your family members?" I crossed my arms, sensing that this wouldn't go smoothly.

"It wasn't a request." The anger I'd been fighting to suppress was racing to the surface, and I had the strangest sensation of my eyes flickering. Some of the Protectors gasped. I had no idea why, and at this point, I didn't care. Patrice, for her part, continued to regard me coolly.

"You've made it quite clear that you want nothing more to do with us, Isolde. Why should we help you now?" She sat back in her seat, crossing her arms, and I noticed that a few others raised their eyebrows and looked at her.

"Is that how the elders are going to play this? Seriously?"

Watching the other Order Members look back and forth between us, it would have been almost comical if I wasn't ready to jump across the table and strangle Patrice. Liam moved closer, resting a hand on my shoulder and squeezing it lightly.

"You came here and threatened us, and now you expect us to help you?"

How had I ever felt a connection to this woman? I watched her closely, sensing that behind her bravado was a very healthy dose of fear.

I allowed a slow, dangerous smile to pass over my face.

"Oh, believe me, Patrice. I still have every intention of bringing the Order to its knees. That wasn't an idle threat," I said, snapping the fingers on my right hand, and everyone gasped as a ball of fire appeared in the palm of my hand. A few of the Protectors scrambled out of their seats, and Liam moved with lightning speed to stand before me, his hands on my shoulders and his eyes wide. I shook my head at him and indicated that he should move. He reluctantly did so, moving to stand behind me, his body pressed close, keeping his hands on my shoulders. While he had known about my fire ability, this was the first time he'd seen me summon it without a candle, and I could tell he was a little shaken at this revelation.

"I started working on this a few weeks ago. Some of my amazing powers that you were all promising would arrive. I have a few secrets up my sleeve. Wanna see mine, Patrice?" I let my lips curl up into a sneer, and Patrice had the sense to look alarmed. "I'll show you mine if you show me yours." I waved the flame around in the air, enjoying myself while those closest to me recoiled further. "If you expect me to stop whatever is coming next, the Order will protect my family, and they will jump through whatever hoops I make them jump through. You know why?"

Liam was still tense behind me, but I couldn't worry about him right now, focusing all my attention on the other people in the room. On one woman in particular.

Patrice's eyes widened, but she cleared her throat before answering. "Why?"

"Because you fucking owe me." I glared at her for a moment before snapping my fingers again, extinguishing the flame.

I felt all eyes on me, and I relished the fear I could feel coming off them all in waves. "Besides, you all kept telling me how I was the most powerful amongst the Order... Do you really want to test me?" So many looks were exchanged, and as one, the Protectors turned to look at Patrice. She still hadn't taken her eyes off my face, but she must have felt the weight of all those eyes staring at her, and after a beat, she nodded her head slowly. The others sighed collectively, and Liam relaxed slightly, his grip on my shoulders easing a fraction.

"Now, besides protecting my family, I have another question." I moved to the seat opposite Patrice's, which Damon usually sat in—the two heads of the table. Liam moved to stand beside me, presenting a united front.

"I want to know how the elders managed to keep the details of both prophecies from Liam for all these years." I leaned back in the chair and crossed my arms, continuing to stare at Patrice closely.

"I'm interested to know the answer to this, also?" Gerard spoke up, and Patrice raised an eyebrow when she looked at him. "We are all intrigued to know what other secrets the elders have kept from us." He gestured around at the others at the table, and it was my turn to raise an eyebrow when the others nodded.

"Looks like we aren't the only ones pissed off, Patrice," Liam said from beside me, speaking for the first time since we'd entered the room.

Patrice looked around the room, appearing to realise that the elders may not be as in control as they thought.

"No one in here is required to be here, Patrice. The Order is meant to be a family and focus on protecting people. But this last week, we've realised that that is not necessarily true, and we want answers." Barbara entered the conversation now, and I couldn't resist the smirk that crossed my lips. I may have lost faith in the elders, but the other Order members seemed to be on my side after all. Patrice shot her a stunned look. I knew she and Barbara were close, and she undoubtedly felt her disappointment the most.

Silence descended over the room as everyone continued to look at Patrice, waiting for answers. Finally, she sat back in her seat and sighed.

"Firstly, I have never intentionally worked against anyone in this room. We have always been working towards the same cause – keeping humanity safe from vampires and finding a way to end the war between the bloodlines. Yes, the elders kept the full details of the prophecy from the rest of the Order, but that is because they hoped they had interpreted it wrong and that we wouldn't have to sacrifice Order members and their families to achieve it."

I couldn't hide the snort of derision that escaped from my lips, and Liam once again placed his hand on my shoulder.

"Spare us the line, Patrice." Liam's voice held the same level of scepticism that I felt, and I could tell from the looks on the faces of the others that many of them felt the same way.

"Whilst it isn't a line, I will answer your question. When you came of age, Liam, and joined the Order as a daywalker with the ability to read minds, the elders at the time were wary of where your allegiances might lie.

The decision was made to have a spell cast that guarded the elders' minds so that certain thoughts and pieces of information didn't end up in the hands of the daywalkers. We know how they feel about us. They've never made a secret of it." Liam crossed his arms now, and I could tell this was not going down well with him.

"Conveniently, though, those thoughts and pieces of information related to myself and, later, Isolde. And my brother... And her sister." Liam said, nodding towards me before continuing. "Certainly wouldn't want that information getting into the wrong hands, would we? And what of Alana? How the fuck did the Order believe that the prophecy was about her when she wasn't a twin?" I hadn't even thought about that before now. I was interested to see what Patrice said.

"She was. But she and her sister were split up in the foster system after the fire that killed the rest of her family. The elders lost track of her, though," Daniel spoke for the first time, answering instead of Patrice.

I could still feel his anger but noted that it seemed to be directed at Patrice, not Liam or myself.

"More fucking lies?!" Liam glared at Patrice, who looked uncomfortable.

"I didn't make the rules, Liam."

"You didn't push back against them, either! We all trusted you! You. Not the other elders. *You.*" He pointed a finger at her, and she recoiled slightly. "This group has followed *you* from place to place. Because *you* were our family."

The anger and betrayal that Liam had been bottling up for the past week and a half had finally surfaced, and it broke my heart to hear it in his voice. I put my hand up beside me, and he took it without hesitation, lacing our fingers together and resting them on my shoulder.

Patrice's face dropped when she finally realised the true impact of her deceit and the pain it had caused, and I saw her deflate a little more while tears formed in her eyes. She looked around the room again, taking in how hurt everyone was. It wasn't just anger that had everyone lashing out. It was the lack of trust that she'd had in them and the betrayal of the confidence that they had placed in her.

Barbara cleared her throat beside me, and we all looked at her when she spoke up. "I think we all need to process everything. And Patrice, it would be best if you found a way to make this all right again. We all need each other now. Everything is about to go to hell in a handbasket, from what I've been able to decipher of the Gemini Prophecy after reading it this week." She looked at me. "The flood was just the start. We have no idea what else is coming, and I'd rather we all be united once it starts." Around the table, the others exchanged looks, and a few nodded. Liam's eyes found mine, and he squeezed my hand.

"Agreed." I looked back at Patrice, who nodded at me. "But, I can't extend that courtesy towards Damon."

"Damon has already realised that he has lost your trust and won't be an issue. He has left the Manor for the time being." A mixture of relief and disgust washed over me, and I knew I'd been right not to trust him. At least Patrice had remained to face the consequences of her actions.

"I won't be answering to the elders any further. They have lost the right to have a say in any decisions Liam and I make." Patrice nodded again, and I rose to my feet, squeezing Liam's hand when he stepped forward.

"Isolde and I will be back. We won't stay here, and I need time to process all this."

I knew how much it pained Liam to have learned that so many secrets had been purposely kept from him over the past five hundred years, and he no doubt wondered what else he hadn't been told. He looked at me again, and I nodded before allowing him to lead me out of the room.

We drove back to the house in silence, both lost in thought. I followed Liam inside and accepted the glass of blood he handed me wordlessly, having been doing my level best to ignore the burning that had been building in my throat since last night. He watched me drink it, then silently poured me another glass. I watched him closely, becoming concerned at the look on his face and the fact that he hadn't uttered a single word since we walked out of the Manor.

"I feel like there's more going on with you than what you've been telling me, isn't there?"

And there it was. The question I had been so hoping he wouldn't ask. That I'd been avoiding because I didn't want to become another person who kept things from loved ones.

I put the glass down without drinking and looked at him.

"What do you want to know?" I asked while he leaned back against the bench and crossed his arms, his eyes searching mine.

"Whatever it is that you're not telling me." He didn't know what I was keeping from him, and I wondered briefly how much I should tell him.

"Connor spoke to me in a dream the other night." I left out that I also seemed to be seeing Aurora's memories. I figured it was best to keep it to myself until I worked that part out.

"He did what?!" Liam asked loudly, and I felt my stomach flip at the expression on his face.

"Well, I'm pretty sure it *wasn't* a dream. He spoke to me and said he was testing out the connection he'd forged between us." I wrapped my arms around myself while he silently processed what I'd said.

"He told you he'd forged a connection with you... And you didn't tell me?"

"I didn't want to hurt you or say anything more until I knew what it meant." He let out a breath and straightened up.

"I think I need to get some air. I'll be back in a while." He strode back through the door we'd not long entered and left me standing alone in the kitchen.

I wasn't sure how to handle this. We'd never fought before, at least not since we'd been together, and my heart hurt to know I had caused him more distress. I could have returned to the office and his journals, but I didn't want to delve further into his memories. It felt like an invasion of his privacy after the conversations we'd just had. Although I couldn't control the flashes, I didn't need to do anything to cause them to appear unnecessarily.

Chapter Fourteen

L IAM EVENTUALLY RETURNED, BUT the distance between us remained, even when we fell asleep beside each other. But whilst we slept, we gravitated together, and I awoke in his arms. He didn't speak when he did kiss my forehead before getting up, leaving me with the empty feeling I'd been battling ever since he'd gone for his walk yesterday. When it was time to leave, I silently followed him to the car, and we began the drive to the Manor.

When we were halfway there, Liam finally broke his silence, and I jumped when he cleared his throat. I had been staring out the window, trying to deal with my emotions.

"Once we leave the manor today, we need to pause. You're still going through the transition with the blood memories, and I want to put a little distance between everyone and us until we can fully understand who knows what and the things that are coming."

Relieved that he had finally spoken, I nodded. I didn't have an issue with hiding out at the house together and ignoring all the bullshit for a little longer. Especially if it meant we could get past this wall that Liam had built up around himself. I'd not experienced any more unwanted visits from Connor, and the less chance of seeing Aurora and Will right now, the better I'd feel. I just needed a time-out before I eventually exploded.

Liam drove into the underground car park for the first time since my transition, a sign that he at least wasn't intending to leave immediately, and I followed him into the elevator.

Once the doors closed, he smacked the emergency stop button before turning to press me back against the wall, bringing his mouth down to mine and kissing me hungrily. A thrill ran through me, and I responded immediately. I pulled him against me while I stroked his tongue with my own. I could feel that he was already hard against my abdomen, and he lifted me off the ground to sit on the handrail. I wrapped my legs around him, pulling him into me. I gasped when he ground himself against my centre. I reached between us and undid his fly as his mouth moved down to my throat, and I moaned with each movement between us. I pushed his boxers down and pumped my hand along his shaft while he groaned into my neck. I felt a shudder run through him when I squeezed lightly and continued guiding my hand up and down. I let my head fall back against the wall while he rubbed my sensitive bundle of nerves through the fabric of my underwear, and both of us began breathing heavily. I was very grateful for my limited wardrobe options, having been left with only the dresses I'd left at the Manor. He lowered his finger to push my underwear aside and inserted two fingers inside me to ensure I was ready for him, crushing his mouth to mine when I moaned loudly.

I used the hand still holding him to guide his tip to my entrance. Once we were aligned, he pushed inside me with one hard thrust of his hips, and I gasped against his lips. With both hands on my hips, he started moving inside me with long, deep strokes while my inner walls clamped around him, my orgasm exploding through me.

"Fuck." He growled into my neck when I began moving with him, the intense pleasure giving way to another wave as my next orgasm quickly grew. I could feel him getting closer to his release, and I reached a hand up to push his head down, guiding his mouth closer to my neck, urging him to bite down, knowing that one bite would send us both over the edge together.

He didn't hesitate. I saw stars when he bit into me and began to suck, intense pleasure rolling over me. His muffled moans mingled with mine when I felt his release run through him. A few more strokes and we collapsed back against the wall together, our breathing heavy.

Removing his mouth from my throat, his forehead met mine.

"Don't keep secrets from me, okay?" He asked, and I nodded as I kept my eyes locked on his. We stayed that way for a moment before I finally let go of his hips and shifted my weight from the handrail. I let my feet fall back to the floor, though his hands gripped my hips until I regained my balance.

With one final kiss, we righted our clothes. Liam looked much calmer when he hit the emergency button again, leaning against the wall beside me and holding my hand while the elevator began moving again.

I couldn't keep the grin from my lips, especially when the door opened to Barbara standing before us, one eyebrow raised and a slight smile on her face. She looked us both up and down, taking in our casual stance, and her gaze lingered on the mostly healed bite mark on my neck before snorting as she turned and walked away. Liam and I exchanged a look and burst out laughing.

Patrice had been busy in the past twenty-four hours, and the spells to cloak each of my family members' homes had been performed. More Order members had begun to arrive from overseas, and I was introduced to them while they sat around the now full conference table, although Damon remained absent. Once again, I was revered by people who had spent years awaiting my birth and subsequent introduction to our mad world.

Ainslie was present, along with a few others who assisted the Order from time to time. I embraced my best friend, still wary about having her mixed up in all of this, but I was selfishly relieved to have someone from my old life to experience this with. She had been brought up to speed on everything that was going on and had volunteered to be on one of the teams that were going to be protecting my family. As someone who was practically a family member anyway, she would be staying with my parents and Briseis for now.

I let Liam do the talking for us today, and once he'd given his orders on how the protection details on my family should run, he waved his hand in my direction.

"Isolde and I are going to step away for a few days. She needs to focus on getting through the transition with the blood memories and harness these new powers before we can face whatever is coming next." I waited for the protests to start, expecting the Order to want us where they could keep an eye on us, to control us. But Patrice simply nodded.

And just like that, I suddenly had no expectations placed upon me. It felt like a weight had been lifted from my shoulders. For the past few months, I had been at the mercy of others' demands on my time. Not having anyone to answer to, even if just for a short amount of time, was something I was not going to say no to.

When we left the Manor, I expected we'd head back to the house and lock ourselves away for a few days or weeks. Instead, Liam began driving us out of the city, and I looked at him expectantly.

"I thought a change of scenery might do us both some good. We might never get a chance at a real vacation together, so this is the best I can offer. I've found us a cottage to stay in at Stanthorpe, no one else around." He raised my hand to his lips when I smiled over at him.

"That sounds amazing. Exactly what we both need right now." I settled myself into my seat, getting comfortable for the few hours it would take us to get there, and closed my eyes, eventually drifting off to sleep.

I closed the front door and looked down the empty street before me, aware of the sounds of rioting not far away. I was still determining how long we could remain in this house while the common people led an uprising against the aristocracy.

The day before, I had been amongst the crowd when the guillotine had dropped upon the neck of a King, something I wasn't sure I'd ever see. Eve had wisely remained absent, having seen the signs growing and stepping away from the world of the French monarchy. The less attention we brought to ourselves now, the better. But I needed to ensure that the members of the Order were safe and had begun to ready themselves to leave this city behind. I hadn't been staying with them recently, having fallen back into bed with Eve, and it was easier to avoid the Order when these urges came over me.

I shook the image of Eve bent over before me while I pounded into her from my mind, and I began the short walk to the current property that the Order had glamoured to hide their headquarters. They were to start the move to the new world on the next available ship, and I was unsure if I would be joining them or remaining with Eve's family for the time being. Vampiric activity remained strong here, but there had been reports of attacks in the newly established United States of America, so the decision had been made to abandon Paris for the time being to protect those in New York. At least here, more daywalkers were present to control the nightwalkers.

A commotion in the alleyway I had just walked past brought my musings to a halt, and I veered off course, turning back towards it, my hand on the stake strapped to my thigh beneath my long coat.

My eyes immediately fell upon a couple pressed back against the wall, the man thrusting deep with his mouth pressed against the woman's neck. Believing I had stumbled upon a couple amid a lovers tryst or perhaps a man partaking of the company of a woman he had paid for, I turned to leave the alley once more, but a movement nearby caused me to pause and look closer. I grew wary when my brother stepped from the shadows, not having noticed my presence.

"Perhaps don't kill her, Adam. We don't need the fucking Order beating down our door again." His tone was

bored, and the man who was rutting away turned to look over his shoulder, and I noted with resignation it was indeed Adam. He growled at Connor, holding the woman against the wall, her throat already gleaming with blood from where he had begun feeding whilst he thrust into her with hard, powerful motions. She was already close to death, her head lolling to the side and her eyes closed. I was disgusted and reached for the stake again but stopped when Connor stepped forward and punched Adam in the face instead. He reeled backwards, and the woman slid to the ground. He jumped to his feet and launched himself towards my twin. Connor raised a hand, and Adam halted before making contact, his feral features going slack. I stayed hidden in the shadows, watching Connor move closer and glare into Adam's face.

"Get your shit under control. You have been leaving a trail of bodies, and I am tired of cleaning up after you. You have become sloppy, and the coven is becoming far too crowded with all the newborns waking up." His voice was low and deadly, and I noticed how his jaw clenched while he stared down the creature before him. This interaction was so strange, and I didn't understand why my brother was acting this way, but Adam nodded, his mind seemingly under the control of whatever hold Connor held over him. They melted into the darkness, and I approached the woman to check if she was still alive. Finding a faint pulse, I took her in my arms and carried her with me while I continued to the Manor. I handed her over to the healers to ensure she survived the night while trying to make sense of everything I had just witnessed.

The memory dissolved around me, but instead of returning to reality, I stood again in the room where I had last seen Connor.

"Interesting... I wasn't aware that my brother had witnessed that particular exchange." The man himself was sitting in the armchair, swirling amber liquid that I assumed was whiskey casually around in the thick crystal glass that he held in his hand. I took in his expression, and I could feel the waves of exhaustion rolling off him, which surprised me. I wasn't aware that nightwalkers could feel this way.

"I'm sure there is plenty about Liam you are unaware of, Connor." I moved to the wall opposite him, leaning back with my arms crossed, my eyes fixed on him should he make any sudden moves.

"I'm sure there is, like how he can keep a woman like yourself so satisfied. I can smell him all over you. How are my brother's skills between the sheets? I bet he learned a lot from Eve over the years. I hear she's insatiable." He smirked, and I could tell he was attempting to goad me into a reaction while he took a mouthful of his drink, holding my gaze over the rim of the glass.

"I must thank her for those lessons, then. Because he truly knows how to make me scream." I refused to allow Connor to gain the upper hand, and he laughed, his eyes flashing between the piercing blue and the brown I had noticed so many times.

"Oh, you came to play, didn't you, Isolde? I do like that. You've got spirit. The Order hasn't managed to turn you into one of their mindless drones just yet." He placed the glass on the table beside him and rose, coming closer. I tensed, but he stopped a few feet away and crossed his arms

while he looked me over. His eyes moved slowly up my body, his gaze appreciative, before settling to look into my own.

"He truly has done well for himself, that brother of mine. Your sister is also something and knows her way around the bedroom, but you... He's almost outdone himself." I didn't need the image of my sister and Connor together that flashed through my mind, and Connor continued to smirk while I looked at him with disgust. "Didn't you know that your sister likes to be shared? She and Will have been busy since she awoke. Inviting anyone who will join them to share their bed. She is quite the screamer herself."

"What do you want, Connor?" I refused to give him the reaction he wanted, and he laughed again, closing the distance between us. He raised his hand and twirled a lock of my hair around his finger, and I held myself still, unsure if he could hurt me in this hellscape he had created between our minds. He raised my hair to his nose and inhaled deeply.

"Do you like to be shared, Isolde?" His eyes held me transfixed, and I inhaled sharply at the unexpected attraction rising within me. I swallowed hard. He began running the fingers of his other hand lightly up my arm. I fought the urge to close my eyes and lose myself to his touch.

"You're not Liam," I said, more as a reminder to my traitorous body, and Connor's eyes flashed again.

"No, I'm not my brother Isolde. I'm something much more." He stepped even closer, and I struggled to keep myself from gasping when the tip of his nose grazed the side of my neck. The hairs on my arms raised at the sensation, and I couldn't bring myself to push him away when his lips settled close to my ear, caging my body in with his hands pressed against the wall on either side of my head. Although no part

of him touched me, I could feel my body screaming for more. I willed myself to take control of the situation, but I felt the desire ripping through me.

"You're using your powers," I said, trying to convince myself, and he let out a low chuckle while he leaned in closer.

"No, I'm not... this is all you. You want this. You're craving what you know I can do for you." His words were a low whisper in my ear, and somehow, with a resolve I wasn't aware I was capable of, I placed my hand on his chest and pushed him away from me. He stepped back without resisting and grinned at me while I panted heavily.

"I don't know what your fucked up end goal is here, but Liam is the only brother I want." He cocked his head to the side while he took in my words, so at odds with how my body was still reacting to his closeness.

"For now. We'll see what will happen once you see more of the memories. But until then...." He crossed the distance at super speed and kissed me hungrily, my body yielding immediately, much to my absolute disgust. He ended the kiss and pressed his forehead to mine. "Until then, Isolde, that's just a taste of what we could be together." I was left feeling cold when he disappeared, and the connection dissolved.

Without waking, I settled into a fitful sleep until I was awoken by the sensation of the car slowing down. I opened my eyes when Liam brought the car to a stop in front of a cute, cosy-looking cottage nestled amongst a lovely little garden at the end of a long driveway. No other buildings were within eyesight, exactly like Liam promised, and I breathed in the smell of the countryside.

"Did you sleep okay? You were mumbling a little over there." Liam surveyed my face, and I shook my head.

"Just another memory. Nothing important, though." There was no way I could tell him what had just occurred between myself and Connor. He didn't need to know that his brother could control my mind and make me do things I *did not* want to do.

Whatever you need to tell yourself, Isolde. Connor's words rang in my mind, and I willed myself to shut out the memory of his mouth on mine and how my body had reacted. To be in this moment with Liam and ignore all the crap for as long as possible. But when I exited the car, my body gave one last involuntary shudder at the memory of Connor's hand on my arm, trailing his fingers so gently up to my neck. It was hard to remind myself that the man was a creature of pure evil in that moment of tenderness.

I pushed the memory from my mind, jumping slightly when Liam's arms wrapped around me from behind before allowing myself to sink back into his embrace. We stood staring out at the paddocks and the herd of cattle spread out before us, munching on grass and utterly ignorant of the world's ways.

"Thank you for bringing me here," I said quietly, and Liam squeezed me before turning me to face him.

"My motives may not have been entirely noble." He lifted my chin and kissed me softly.

"No? What other motives could you possibly have? I thought you were all about pure thoughts and the good of others," I whispered against his lips before shrieking when he grabbed me and threw me over his shoulder.

"Not when you're wearing that dress, Isolde. Then I want to do all sorts of dirty things to you." I felt my heart rate pick up at the change in his tone when he pushed the door open with his foot and carried me inside.

Chapter Fifteen

MOVING THROUGH THE COTTAGE to the bedroom, Liam used the hand that wasn't holding me in place to reach up under my dress, showing me how dirty those thoughts were with his fingers. Moaning, I did nothing to stop him from tossing me on the bed. He leaned over and claimed my lips while he continued working his fingers between my legs, rubbing over the fabric of my underwear, and I writhed under his touch.

"What do you say, Isolde? Should I keep it pure with you right now?" He whispered against my lips while I rocked my hips against his hand.

"No. Definitely no pure thoughts and actions here, please," I said breathlessly, and he chuckled, moving to lie beside me without moving his hand away. He looked down at me, continuing to tease me, and I moaned again. "God, Liam, please. I need more."

"I love it when you beg." His voice had taken on a rough, commanding tone, and I felt it right down to my toes.

"Please, Liam. Make me come."

His eyes lit up while I continued to beg him, rewarding me by shifting the fabric aside and pushing his finger inside of me, his thumb moving to continue what his finger had started. He knew my body so well that I was on the edge almost immediately, and he continued to hold my gaze as my back arched up off the bed and the orgasm crashed through me. He kept going, his hand moving faster, pulling several more from me, while I cried out repeatedly, overwhelmed by the sensations rocking through me and the intense look in his eyes.

When I came down from the latest orgasm, he pulled his hand away finally and began sliding my underwear down my legs, tossing them over his shoulder.

"Get on your knees." He growled, and if I hadn't already come several times, I swore I would have combusted at those words. This was a side that I had never seen in my usually controlled, calm lover. I hadn't realised how much he liked this dress, but after our encounter in the elevator earlier, and now this, I knew I needed to wear it all the time.

Following his command, my heart sped up with anticipation when I heard him undo his belt. Within seconds, he pushed inside me with one quick thrust, and I cried out again. He leaned over me to wrap his arm around my chest and pull me upright against him. With his other hand pressed firmly over my overstimulated bundle of nerves, his thrusts pushed me to rub against his fingers with each movement. The hand he had been using to hold me against his chest slid inside the low neckline of my dress and squeezed my breast, pinching my nipple before moving to my throat, thrusting harder into me. My eyes rolled back, and my head fell back against his shoulder.

"That's it, Isolde. Scream my name."

I gasped as my heightened senses became over-whelmed again, and I did, indeed, scream his name.

"Fuck, Liam. Don't stop!"

"Wasn't planning on it."

I hadn't thought it was possible, but he moved his hips faster, and I raced towards the edge again.

"Fuck, Isolde. You feel so good." He sunk his teeth into my neck and held me tight around the throat while I continued to whimper. He kept going, his lips pressed to my skin while he fucked me hard, and I toppled over into oblivion, finally taking him over the edge with me, our cries mingling together.

He held me firmly against him, my body limp in his arms while I fought to catch my breath. Once we had the energy to untangle from each other, I lay back on the bed, snuggling into his side while he wrapped his arm around me.

"Who was that? This dress seems to bring out a whole different side of you." I trailed my finger over his chin, turning his head to bring his gaze to mine. He studied my face closely, moving to press a tender kiss to my forehead and breathe in my scent.

"I just had a bit of a realisation yesterday when I went for a walk. I was holding back from you, too." He ran his hand up and down my side, holding my gaze.

"What do you mean holding back?"

For a brief moment, I worried about what awful truths were about to come tumbling from his beautiful lips.

"When you were human, I didn't allow myself to unleash that side of my nature fully. I know talking about Eve is a sore spot for both of us, but it was only when I was with her that I could fully let go because I wasn't afraid of breaking her."

I opened my mouth to speak, but he raised his other hand to place a finger over my lips. I bit his finger, and he laughed.

"I realised last night that I no longer have to hold back with you. I don't *want* to hold back with you anymore. Can you handle that?" He asked, and I stared at him for a moment.

"Are you kidding? I fucking loved that. I craved that."

He pulled me in close and kissed me hungrily.

"Good, because I'm not done." He pushed my arms up over my head, using his belt to clasp my hands to the bedhead before kissing his way down my body. I gasped when he showed me just how much he had been holding back before, working my body in ways I didn't know were possible and ruining me for all other men.

Several hours later, I sat in the kitchen and watched Liam make dinner, having gone to get some supplies in town while I took a shower. Seeing him standing before the stove, shirtless in jeans and barefoot, made me painfully aware that this was the most relaxed I'd ever seen him in the eight months we'd known each other. It was as though getting away from Brisbane had flicked a switch within him. I wished we could just stay here, ignoring all responsibilities, and just be Liam and Isolde, the couple, rather than holding the fate of the world in our hands.

"Have I told you lately how much I love you?" I asked, and he looked over his shoulder, shooting me the sexiest smirk I'd ever seen.

"Is this because I'm feeding you?" He asked, and I pretended to think for a moment before answering.

"Maybe that's it. Couldn't be because seeing you this relaxed is doing all sorts of things to my insides right now." He laughed while putting our meals together and bringing me my plate. He placed it on the bench before me and came around to wrap his arms around me, while I stayed sitting on the high bench seat.

"I do feel so much lighter here, you're right. Let's just stay here forever." He said into my hair, his lips brushing my ear.

"Oh yes please, I'm one hundred percent on board with that plan." I hugged him back, before allowing him to step away to go and get his food.

"How about this for a plan? We survive all this bullshit coming our way, and we move out here and just forget about everything else?"

I could tell that only a small part of him was joking, and I studied him closely.

"You're on." We both began eating, enjoying the quiet and this brief pause in reality, almost like we were two regular people in love and not part of some elaborate plan to end a supernatural war.

Chapter Sixteen

THAT EVENING, ONCE MY body was entirely spent from all of Liam's attention, the blood memories began flowing in earnest. Memories from Liam and Aurora came flooding through, one after the other, as though all I had needed was to step away from all the stress at home before the floodgates could open. Liam kept busy, ensuring my needs for blood and food were met. But I still couldn't bring myself to tell Liam that I was seeing Aurora's memories along with his own.

He was also more than willing to make sure my needs for him were sufficiently met during any moments of awareness between the memories, and our hunger for one another only grew stronger with each shared moment. By the end of the fourth day, I felt like I had experienced every significant moment in their lives. Thankfully, Liam's dedication to ensuring that I experienced countless orgasms kept me from completely losing grip on myself and my reality outside of the memories belonging to both my twin sister and my vampire lover. I could have done without experiencing every sexual encounter they had both had, finding the ones between Aurora and Will particularly hard to stomach, closely followed by the many interactions between Liam and Eve. The only silver lining was that it was comforting to know that although his number of sexual conquests had been very high over the last five hundred years, none held the intensity and love I knew he had experienced with me.

Although it was summer, the nights were surprisingly cool, and we had a fire in the fireplace. I stared into the flames now while I lay my head on Liam's chest, my bare leg draped across his hips while we enjoyed the quiet contentment that had fallen over us after our latest round of lovemaking. Liam's eyes were closed, his hand running slowly up and down my back.

"How are you handling all of this? I know these past few weeks have been especially hard for you, too." I said, and he let out a breath, opening his eyes to look at me. He brought his hand to a stop at the back of my neck and began massaging it gently.

"It's a lot to take in. To have five hundred years of knowledge ripped out from underneath me and find out it was all just a bunch of convenient half-truths and outright lies will take me some time to deal with." He ran the hand on my leg up my side and cupped my breast. "Thank goodness I have you to keep me distracted." His lips curled into a seductive smile, and he lifted his head to kiss me softly. I opened my mouth to him while we began to explore each other's bodies again, the conversation giving way to moans once more.

Hours later, we finally fell into a deep sleep, the days of dealing with stress, and more recently, the relentless flood of memories and lovemaking, leaving us exhausted. Thankfully, my dreams remained Connor-free while I lay wrapped in Liam's arms.

We could have slept for days, but we both jerked awake suddenly in the middle of the night when a sense of dread seeped into our dreams. Liam leapt out of bed, throwing on jeans that lay discarded on the floor and tossing me his shirt while I scrambled over the bed to his side. I yanked the shirt over my head, and we both made our way outside, grabbing our stakes from the side of the bed as we went.

But there was nothing untoward that we could see outside, the absence of any artificial light making the sky appear to stretch out endlessly before us. If it weren't for the sense that something was wrong, I would have been in awe of the fantastic array of stars above us. We remained on alert, back to back, while we surveyed the paddocks around us for any sign of the source of the pit of dread in both our bellies.

Just when I began to believe we were experiencing some weird side effect of days of insufficient sleep, the ground beneath our feet began to tremble slightly. Liam grabbed my hand when the shaking increased rapidly, and we both dropped to the ground, unable to remain upright due to the intense rocking and rolling. I'd never experienced an earthquake before, and if I were still human, I imagined its violence would make me feel sick. As it was, my heightened senses were all over the place, and I curled into a ball, Liam's arms coming around me while we waited for it to stop.

After what felt like forever, the shaking stopped as abruptly as it began, and I slowly opened my eyes, looking around. A few trees had toppled over in the distance, and the cows mooed loudly while they ran around in the paddock. I could relate to their terror. Liam checked me over, and we slowly rose to our feet, hesitant, waiting to see if it was truly over or if any aftershocks would follow.

While we stood there, a shooting star streaked across the sky, closely followed by another. Then another.

Star after star shot overhead, and we stared at the sky, gaping at the amazing display. It was breathtaking to behold, and I would have been happy to take in the beauty of it all if not for the internal alarm shrieking inside of my head, warning me that this was all related to the prophecy and a sign of worse things to come.

Liam looked over at me, the concern I felt mirrored in his eyes while the stars continued to fly across the sky. They didn't stop until it was almost dawn, and we finally went inside, deciding that we should spend this one last day in blissful ignorance before we once more headed back into the abyss of the unknown that we'd left behind.

Thankfully, our final day and night were uneventful, and we reluctantly climbed back into the car and drove back to Brisbane. We had managed to avoid any technology while we were away, and I scanned my phone now, responding to concerned messages from my family members and reading the news to see what the so-called experts had to say about the earthquake and sudden, unexpected meteor shower from the night before. There were dozens of astronomers and seismologists across numerous news sites discussing the events, trying to explain away what had happened, each more fantastical than the next. The fact that the Order hadn't been able to keep this from making the global news channels was sign enough that things were spinning out of control, and everything within me knew that this was related to the prophecy.

"We'd better go straight to the Manor. I want to get a feel for what is going on," Liam said when we reached the city outskirts, and I nodded absently while I scrolled through my phone. We remained silent for the rest of the drive - each lost in our thoughts while we tried to grasp everything happening. I couldn't shake the feeling that the earthquake and meteor shower were just the beginning.

Once Liam parked the car, we entered the elevator, and I smirked a little at the memory of the last time we'd been inside. But that smirk disappeared when the doors opened, and we saw who was standing in the lobby of the Manor.

"What the fuck..." Liam's words trailed off when he took in Eve and Ronson's presence. They were standing casually before a very agitated Patrice, and I could tell this visit was unwelcome.

"There you are," Eve said, looking bored while Patrice wrung her hands, biting her lip as she looked to Liam for assistance.

"How the hell are you here?" Liam demanded. Besides Liam and now myself, as far as I was aware, no other vampires, daywalkers included, were meant to be able to find this place.

Eve snorted.

"The Order has never been able to keep me out. I just chose never to enter their precious inner sanctum," she said, and Patrice went still beside her. I could tell that this was news to her. A small part of me took some satisfaction in knowing that there were still things she didn't know.

Liam was glaring at Eve.

"Why are you here now, then?" He asked, his words dangerously low. I tried not to think of all the times he'd been with the woman before me over the last five hundred years, but I could tell from the smirk on Eve's face that she was well aware of the memories I had been privy to over the last week and a half.

"Now that Isolde is up to speed, it's time for our plans to move along. If you refuse to return to our side, we will be wherever she is," she said with a shrug, and I gaped at her.

"Ridiculous. You can't expect to stay here, surely?" Patrice asked shrilly, and Eve turned ever so slowly to look at her, running her eyes over Patrice with a look of pure disdain.

"We'll do whatever the fuck we like," Ronson spoke this time, one of few things I'd heard him say. Even in Liam's memories, he had rarely spoken. Patrice stepped back, perhaps sensing the danger he presented despite being a daywalker. Eve ignored Patrice and moved closer to where Liam and I stood. Liam moved to stand in front of me.

"Back off, Eve."

Eve huffed a laugh. Over Liam's shoulder, I watched her reach up and pat him gently on the cheek with a smirk.

"Oh, Liam... Dear, dear Liam. I find it amusing that you think either of you have any say in what is about to happen. Your only choice right now is if you will return with us or if we will remain here. But from now on, you *will* be with us." Although we'd had no intention of staying at the Manor anyway, I knew there was no way in hell that Liam would want Eve back at the house, and I could tell he was trying to work out what to do. Sensing that things could get ugly, I stepped around him and looked Eve up and down. I refused to let her revel in the power she held over everyone.

"We will come back to the house for now. But you don't call the shots, Eve. If we want to leave, we will be leaving." Over her shoulder, I could see that Patrice was fighting an internal war against the relief she felt that Eve would be leaving, but unhappy that we would also be leaving with her. The Order wanted to maintain control of the situation, but they couldn't win against a vampire who was thousands of years old and apparently could enter the doors of the Manor whenever she chose.

Eve turned her smirk on me now, and I glowered at her.

"Whatever you need to tell yourself, Isolde." She placed a hand on Liam's chest, almost as though staking her claim over him. I fought the urge to smack her hand away, aware that she was toying with me, attempting to goad me. Liam stood still beside me, his hands clenched into fists and his jaw tense.

"See you both at the house. You have one hour."

I didn't want to know what would happen if we didn't comply.

Once Eve and Ronson had swept out the door, we headed into the comms room to work out what the Order had managed to find out about the earthquake and meteor shower we'd witnessed.

"We've had reports of several earthquakes worldwide in areas that don't normally experience movement," Barbara said to Liam while she searched the internet for information.

I continued conversing with Patrice.

"Have there been any other events since I turned? Besides the flood here?" I asked her, trying to bring her out of the distracted state she'd been in since Eve had dropped the bomb that she'd been able to get through the glamours. "Patrice! I need you to focus." Her eyes snapped back to me.

"Sorry. Yes, there have been. The flooding isn't just contained to Brisbane, though it was the epicentre. Flooding events have been occurring in a steady spread outwards. It's already reached out to Sydney, the Queensland and Northern Territory Borders and as far North as Rockhampton. And this morning, we also started to get reports of New Zealand experiencing events. So it's not just Australia now. If we don't work out how to stop all of this, we predict that the entire planet will be affected within several weeks."

I'm sure the shocked look on Liam's face was mirrored on my own. I think I liked it better when Patrice wasn't speaking.

"Okay... So we've got flooding... Like the biblical flood?"

"Not entirely. The flood in the Bible was from constant rain. There's not been any increased rainfall in these instances. The waters are rising on their own."

"That is quite possibly more terrifying." My mind was reeling, but Liam continued to watch Patrice closely.

"There's more, isn't there?" He asked.

Patrice looked reluctant to say what was running through her mind.

"We've got dormant volcanoes worldwide starting to show signs of life. We think that might be the reason for the earthquakes."

Liam swore under his breath, and I just stared at Patrice.

"How long have we got before everything goes to complete shit?" I asked.

Patrice shook her head.

"Honestly, we have no way of knowing, but we need to work out your role in all of this, or the world will explode in a matter of months if not weeks."

Great... No pressure.

Chapter Seventeen

WHEN WE'D BEEN AT Eve's home the last time, I had only crossed paths with Eve and Ronson. I had seen the room I'd been kept in and the way out of the house. But now that we were back, I realised it was an eerily similar set-up to the Manor. But whilst the Manor was glamoured to look like several run-down houses from the outside, Eve's home wasn't hidden. And it was massive. I'd been too out of it when we were here last time to notice it when we left, but I gaped up at it now, wondering how I'd ever missed this place in all my years in Brisbane.

"She certainly likes to make a statement, doesn't she?" I commented to Liam while we climbed out of my car and stared at the three-storey mansion high up on the hill. Even from the driveway, the view out over the city was impressive. However, it was probably much nicer when the river wasn't raging. It had been two weeks, yet the waters were still flowing fast. The water levels had decreased a little, which was how I'd seen my former home, but it was still much higher than usual. Debris flowed by regularly, and I wondered how long it would continue to flow like this.

Probably until I could sort out this whole "end of days" part of the bloody prophecy.

"Yes, Eve has frequented only the most opulent homes in the time I've known her. As you've no doubt seen." It was the first time Liam had come even close to referencing his shared history with the woman who had turned his life upside down, and I had no desire to discuss it any further. Even now, just thinking about it made my insides boil. I'd never been a particularly jealous person in life. But between being turned into a vampire with heightened emotions and learning that my fiance and sister had been having a multiple-year affair behind my back, I guess jealousy was now just another part of my personality I had to get used to. I felt my eyes flash again like they had when I'd become angry at the Manor in front of everyone, and Liam stared hard at me.

"What?" I didn't like the look on his face. He squinted at me like something was seriously wrong with my face.

"Your eyes..." He trailed off, and I raised a hand to my face.

"What about my eyes?"

He shook his head after a moment.

"I must have imagined it... It just looked like they changed colour for a moment. But that's not possible."

I felt my blood run cold, even though Liam was trying to make it sound like it was no big deal.

"What colour did they change to?"

"They looked brown for a moment. But honestly, I was just seeing things. Eyes don't change colour like that." Liam turned towards the house again and reached out to take my hand. I took it automatically and allowed him to lead the way inside.

Inside my head, though, alarm bells were screaming. He was right. Eyes didn't change like that. But I had seen someone else whose eyes had changed from piercing blue to brown once. And I wasn't loving how the jigsaw in my head was starting to put the pieces into place.

Liam led the way inside without bothering to knock. I'm sure he even considered kicking the door out of frustration with our current situation. Neither of us wanted to be here, but we had little choice. As Liam's sire, Eve had a connection to him and could generally sense wherever he was. It was how she had timed her arrival at the Manor with ours. I hadn't been impressed when Liam had divulged that little tidbit of information on the drive over. He'd explained that it was due to the blood memories. It also meant that we were linked in the same way. I wasn't concerned about that, though. I was preoccupied with the idea that a vampire who was thousands of years old and seemed to care little for humans was tied to my vampire lover.

"Well, Eve, you got your way. We're here." Liam yelled from the foyer, my hand still firmly gripped in his. I could tell that he was doing everything possible to contain his anger.

"Jeez, Liam, settle down." A woman I vaguely recognised from some of his memories appeared at the door to our left, leaning against the door frame with a smirk. She was stunning, with long limbs and deep brown skin that caused her piercing blue eyes to stand out even more than any other vampire I'd met. I detected a trace of an American accent in her voice.

"Screw you, Anika," he said, but there was no malice to his words, and he dropped my hand before going over to sweep her up into a hug.

This was a strange new development. I still hadn't seen everything in his life. Five hundred years was a lot to cram into two weeks' worth of memories, and most of the ones I had seen had involved Eve, Connor or members of the Order. Seeing him be friendly with a daywalker was a little bit of a surprise.

"Welcome back, big brother." She hugged him back tightly before stepping back to look him over. Brother?

"I'd say thanks, but given that I don't want to be here, I'm not sure welcome is the right word," Liam said, the frustration returning to his voice.

"Ah yes, Michael mentioned Eve went off on a little retrieval mission." She finally looked at me, running her eyes over me slowly. "So, this is your girl, huh?"

I wasn't entirely sure I liked how she was looking at me. But Liam hadn't taken on his usual protective stance when someone threatened me, so I held her gaze.

"This is Isolde, yes." Liam turned back towards me, and Anika stepped around him to come and stand before me. I tensed slightly. My experiences with the other daywalkers had not been particularly welcoming, and given this woman chose to spend time with Eve, I wasn't prepared to take any chances with her yet.

She continued to inspect me, and I stared right back, refusing to be intimidated. Finally, a big smile appeared on her face, and I was taken aback at the complete change in her attitude when she swept me up into a huge hug and squeezed tightly. I looked over her shoulder at Liam, my eyebrows raised. He shrugged with a smile.

"I like her," Anika said over her shoulder when she finally let go, and I didn't know what to say.

"Um, thanks?" I was suddenly aware of the burning in my throat and remembered it had been several hours since I'd had blood. I truly hoped the intense urge for blood would pass soon because it was incredibly inconvenient. And I was concerned that sometimes humans looked like a tasty snack.

"You need blood. Come on," Anika said.

I had no idea how they all seemed to know when my need for blood overwhelmed me, but I allowed her to take me by the hand and lead me into a large kitchen towards the back of the house. Liam followed close behind.

"Wow." I stopped short at the door. It was the fanciest kitchen I had ever seen, with top-end appliances, including several stoves and ovens. The fridge even had a touch screen, which I'd never seen before.

"Ronson likes to cook," Anika said over her shoulder while she opened the fridge and pulled out a pitcher that I assumed was filled with blood. I turned slowly to look at Liam, unable to imagine the stoic, silent Ronson as a fancy chef who used all the gadgets in this kitchen. Again, Liam shrugged. He seemed unable to do much more than that now that we were back here. I felt there would be many more revelations while we were here. I wasn't sure how I felt about that.

Anika had been chattering while she poured blood into a fancy glass that looked like it was made of crystal. That didn't surprise me in the slightest. From what I knew about Eve, she enjoyed the finer things in life, and her choice of glassware would be no exception. I tuned in to what Anika said while she handed me the glass.

"The others are all starting to arrive," She said to Liam.

I wondered how many *others* she was referring to, but I needed to deal with the burning in my throat before I could focus on anything else. I drained the glass before handing it back wordlessly to Anika. She raised an eyebrow at me before shooting a look at Liam and pouring me a second glass. "Thirsty little thing, aren't ya?" I drained the second glass, trying not to feel self-conscious at her words.

"The transition has been a bit rough. It's only been a couple of weeks, Anika." Liam admonished her, but she just shrugged and took the glass from me again, popping it in the dishwasher behind her. I was relieved that it wasn't the only bloody glass in there.

"So, house rules." Anika clapped her hands, and Liam rolled his eyes with a sigh. "Watch it, Liam. It's been quite a while since you lived with the family."

I found it interesting that they referred to themselves as a family. From what I'd seen of Liam's memories, he didn't consider them family, preferring to stay with the Order instead.

"First rule. Clean the fuck up after yourselves. Quite a few of us are here now, and while we have a housekeeper, if you leave shit around, you will eventually piss off the wrong person." She raised a hand and held up two fingers. "Second rule. Don't piss anyone off." I waited for the rest of the rules, but that seemed to be it. She looked at us both expectantly and didn't seem surprised when Liam huffed a mocking laugh.

"Given that we were summoned here and informed that we had to stay, I don't give a shit who we piss off, Anika."

Someone cleared their throat behind us, and we turned to see a man with pale skin and deep red hair that was cut short enter the room.

He was well built, like every other daywalker I had met so far, and I figured centuries of fighting evil kept everyone in shape. His blue eyes regarded me closely when he came to stand at Anika's side and slung an arm around her shoulders. He towered over her, standing even taller than Liam.

"So, this is the chosen one." He sounded bored, but I could tell it was an act while he ran his eyes over me. Liam growled a little beside me and pulled me close, almost as though he was reminding this man of his claim over me.

"Don't be an asshole, Anthony. It doesn't suit you." Anika smacked him in the chest, and he rolled his eyes at her.

"What? I can't see what all the fuss is about. She doesn't seem any different to any of the rest of us," he said with a shrug.

"I assure you, Anthony, she is more powerful than any of you." Eve's voice rang out behind us, and Liam tensed up again when she entered the room, followed by Ronson and a man I recognised to be Michael from Liam's memories. I felt like this was probably the closest to a compliment I would ever get from her.

She took in Liam's protective stance beside me and rolled her eyes.

"For fuck's sake, Liam, give it a rest."

I detected what I assumed was some jealousy within her aggravation, and I moved closer to Liam, sliding my arm behind his back while I reached around with the other to slide my hand over his chest, coming to rest over his heart, which I could feel beating steadily. He knew what I was doing and chuckled, covering my hand with his own. I was a mouse toying with a hungry cat, but I didn't care. I was tired of dealing with her bullshit.

"I don't know, Eve... I find it hot," I said, my voice low, and she raised an eyebrow, amusement rippling across her features.

"You wanna play Isolde? Be prepared to give it all you've got." Whilst she talked a big game, I could tell the fact that I wasn't intimidated by her mere presence was frustrating her.

"Who's playing? I've already won." I shrugged, and Ronson gave a low warning growl. I flicked my eyes over him. "Careful, Ronson. I'm more powerful than all of you, remember?" I threw Eve's words back at them, and she narrowed her eyes, assessing me closely.

"I didn't say you were more powerful than me, Isolde. Just more powerful than them." Her words were low and dangerous, and Liam squeezed my hand gently, a warning to maybe stop playing with the cat quite so much. Across the kitchen counter, Anthony laughed loudly.

"Oh, this is going to be fun. Eve, I haven't seen someone get under your skin this much in a while. I approve of your woman, Liam." Anthony said, and Anika smacked his chest again. He rubbed the spot, the hit harder than the last one. "What?"

"You know perfectly well *what.*" She shot him a pointed look, and he shot her a cheeky grin, which she answered with a roll of her eyes. They held each other's gaze for a moment longer, and I watched with interest. Could this be the daywalker couple that Liam had mentioned to me once, that were bonded like we had been? If so, their bond appeared to still be intact, unlike ours.

"As fun as all this is, what do you want, Eve? You've forced us here. Now I want to know why." Liam glared at Eve. She finally shifted her gaze from mine to run her eyes slowly over him.

"You can't be surprised that I want all of my family under this roof. Now that you're little Protector lover is one of us, there is no reason for you to remain with them. I've indulged your little rebellion for far longer than I should have."

I gaped at Eve, unable to believe she would even think that a response like that would slide with Liam after everything I'd witnessed of their interactions over the years.

"Fuck you, Eve," Liam's voice came out in a low growl, which sent a shiver of attraction up my spine.

Yep, right on time.

"Liam, darling, watch your tone when you speak to me. I have allowed you to disrespect me over the centuries, but I am growing tired of it. Do I need to remind you of how truly powerful I am?" Her eyes narrowed dangerously while she looked at him, but Liam wasn't backing down.

"I don't give a shit, Eve. You clearly need us here for some reason, so drop the act. What do you want? Never once in all my years have you insisted that I be here, so why now? What's your endgame?" Liam wasn't going to let it go, and rightly so. He wasn't the only one interested in hearing Eve's response. I eyed her coolly, and she once again held my gaze, an aggravating smirk playing across her lips.

"He's right, Eve. Something smells off. What are you planning?" Anika asked, and I was pleased to see that although Eve had a somewhat inflated ego, most of her *family* wasn't afraid to call her out on her bullshit.

"All in good time, my darlings." Eve turned on her heel and walked gracefully towards the door, followed closely by Ronson and Michael. I assumed that these two were the most loyal of her little lapdogs.

"Is that good time before or after the world implodes around us?" I demanded before she reached the door.

"You'll know soon enough." She didn't even look back, and it took every ounce of my little self-control to keep from racing after her and punching her.

"Fucking woman," Anthony said quietly while he and Liam glared at her retreating, and Anika nodded.

Sighing, Liam turned around to look at them both.

"So, what's the deal these days? Do any of you still head out on patrol? I haven't encountered anyone in the last twenty-six years, but surely you aren't all leaving it up to the Order?"

I raised an eyebrow. In all the time I've known him, the involvement of daywalkers in hunting down night-walker covens had never come up.

Anthony snorted.

"As if we'd leave the fate of the world in the hands of those idiots. Yes, we still patrol. Tonight is our night. Wanna come play?" Anthony grinned, looking between Liam and me.

I looked over at Liam, who nodded. I was interested in watching what the daywalkers did differently and why they felt superior to the Order.

"We'll join you," Liam said, and Anika clapped her hands with a wide smile. She was so bubbly, nothing like I'd expected any daywalkers to act.

"This will be so much fun. And I can't wait to see you in action." She directed this at me, and I wondered what my reputation was amongst the daywalkers. Since transitioning, I hadn't fought any nightwalkers other than the brief exchange with Aurora and Will. I was kind of interested to see what all the fuss was about myself.

"She's not coming just for your enjoyment, Anika," Liam said with a huff, and I patted his chest.

"It's okay. It's only natural that everyone is so interested if that's how Eve talks about me. I hope I can live up to the hype."

Liam's eyebrows were raised, and I shrugged. There was no point denying it, with the constant reminders of my supposed superpowers.

Conversation over, Anika and Anthony left us to our own devices, and Liam gave me a brief tour of the house. He'd spent a week trapped here while I transitioned and had made a point of learning the entire layout whilst skilfully avoiding spending too much time with any of the daywalkers. The house was huge, and I realised there were already quite a few more daywalkers living here than I realised when we'd last been here. All seemed to have varying levels of wariness around Liam and me, which I assumed was due to our connection to the Order. I had known that the daywalkers weren't keen on the Order of the Dragon, but I only saw the full extent of that now. I wondered now why Liam had chosen to remain allied with them, and I voiced this curiosity as we entered the room where I had previously been when I transitioned.

"Honestly, because most daywalkers, whilst nowhere near as bad as nightwalkers, have so little regard for humanity. And I needed the connection with my former self that I felt when I was with the Order." Liam said, closing the door behind him.

We hadn't been assigned a room, so we'd just returned here, figuring this was where we were expected to stay. As long as it was away from Eve, I didn't care.

"And how do you feel now after everything we've learnt the past few weeks?" I went to him and wrapped my arms around his waist while he stood with his back to me, looking out the window. He rubbed my arm before lifting my hand and bringing it to his lips.

"Truthfully? Right now, I feel like the only person I can trust is standing right here with me." I understood how he was feeling, even as I tried to push away the guilt that crept up on me, knowing that even I wasn't being entirely truthful with him. I wasn't ready to deal with the suspicions of what seeing Aurora's memories might mean. Denial was so much easier. So I allowed him to draw the comfort he needed from my embrace and hoped with all my heart that I was wrong.

Chapter Eighteen

L IAM AND I ACCOMPANIED Anika and Anthony later that night, leaving the house on foot after midnight to begin our patrol. Although I'd been a daywalker for nearly two weeks now, I still hadn't put my new abilities to any real test, having focussed instead on the blood memories that were still flooding in, often at the most inopportune times. But now I was a little excited to see what I could do. Before, even though I had been one of the best fighters amongst the humans in the Order, Liam was still faster and stronger than I was. I was interested to see if my advanced skills had continued past the transition. I still had no idea how I was meant to be more powerful than everyone else. And I assumed Eve wouldn't tell me anything until she deemed it the right time. Probably at a time when she could make it as dramatic as possible.

"Hey, newbie. Ready to run?" Anika called back over her shoulder when we were halfway down the street. I knew we were headed down to the large park near South-bank, which was still a bit of a distance away. I had assumed we would be driving, so running there sounded interesting.

"Sure," I responded, but before I'd even finished speaking, Anika and Anthony had become two blurs, moving so fast it was impossible to tell who was who. Liam looked over at me with a grin and took off as well. That left me standing alone. This all occurred in a fraction of a second, and I was stunned. I'd seen Liam move like that before, but to have it happen with so many people at once was a slight shock to the system.

But once that shock wore off, I couldn't wait to try it. I took a deep breath before taking off, running as fast as possible. The world around me turned into nothing more than a blur, and the sensation was exhilarating. It took no effort on my part, and within a minute, I arrived at the park, coming to a halt beside Liam. A distance that would have taken us at least twenty minutes to walk at a regular, human pace, and we'd done it within a minute.

"Why on earth do you ever bother driving anywhere?!" I asked him, and he smirked.

"I only ever drove when you were with me, remember? You were the slow-ass one." I gasped at him in mock outrage and tapped his arm. Anika and Anthony were watching us closely but didn't say anything. They retook the lead, and Liam and I followed while we began moving amongst the shadows of the large trees around the park. This park had had a reputation for years as not being the safest at night, but I'd never lived nearby, so it hadn't been on my radar. But now I could understand where the reputation had come from. There were many homeless people, some in tents, with others sleeping on benches and under trees, all of whom I was sure that the police and general public thought were the problem, refusing to acknowledge the societal issues that had led to these people sleeping here.

But the real problem was the nightwalkers I could now sense prowling nearby. These people were perfect prey, and seeing how vulnerable they were out here was so sad because of how society viewed those down on their luck. Only a few people would have noticed if these people had gone missing. And that was concerning on so many levels. How many people had Connor and Adam recruited to their side just by preying on those so often overlooked by the authorities? And worse, the Order hadn't been focussing on these areas either. I was starting to understand why the daywalkers had such a low opinion of the Order.

"Do you patrol this park every night?" I asked quietly, and Anika nodded.

"Yes, this one and many others. It's not the highly populated areas that are the problem. Some nightwalkers might venture into places like the Valley or the city to pick off drunk revellers when they stumble home, but these are the areas where the nightwalkers truly lurk."

I looked at Liam to see his reaction to this information and his take on it, but he shook his head, indicating that now wasn't the time for this conversation. I nodded and went back to scanning the area. A movement in the corner of my eye caught my attention, and I turned to see a nightwalker that I recognised as one of Adam's followers moving towards a sleeping figure on a nearby park bench. He had been present at the restaurant when I'd first come face to face with Connor and Aurora in her current state. His build alone was enough to put a Rugby player to shame, built like a brick wall but moving with the fluid grace of a vampire.

Anthony was already on him before I'd fully registered his presence, having noticed him whilst Anika was talking to me. He moved with such silent precision that the nightwalker was completely surprised when Anthony leapt onto him from the shadows. He had no time to react before Anthony ripped his head from his shoulders with powerful force, and I was both impressed and disgusted at the same time. Patrolling with the Order had been different from this. They'd had to rely on their weapons, and each interaction with a nightwalker had been almost like a fight to the death. But the daywalkers' powers matched those of the nightwalkers. I wondered why the Order even bothered.

I watched, fascinated, while Anthony hefted the body of the nightwalker onto his shoulders with ease, grabbing the head in his free hand from the ground and wandering casually back over to us. The person sleeping on the bench hadn't even stirred.

"What are you going to do with that?" I indicated towards the body draped across Anthony's rather broad shoulders. He shrugged, and it was almost comical watching the headless body bob up and down behind his head. Almost.

"I figured I'd set it on fire. It's what we usually do. We just need to find somewhere less obvious to do it. I can't have the cops stumbling across a burning body." Anthony said.

Liam looked over at me with a raised eyebrow. I winked at him.

"I think I can help with that," I said with a grin.

Anthony looked confused, but the three of them followed me while I led the way, stopping amongst some low bushes. I indicated that Anthony should put the body on the ground, and he did so, exchanging a look with Anika after he dumped it unceremoniously. Anika just shrugged, having no idea what was about to happen. I hoped that my shielding abilities had survived the transition the same as my fire abilities, as I'd not yet thought to test them, and it would make this rather embarrassing if I couldn't follow through.

The others stayed behind me while I focussed on the body. I'd never had an audience other than Liam when I performed magic. I tried not to feel self-conscious with three pairs of eyes boring a hole into my back when I brought my arms up to waist height and closed my eyes, taking a deep breath while centring myself.

"Hide and protect me," I said aloud and was relieved to feel the power ripple through my body when the air around me began to crackle with magic. I heard all three of them draw sharp breaths behind me, and I knew I'd succeeded in becoming invisible to them. Now for the more complicated part of expanding the protective bubble to include them. With my eyes still closed, I concentrated on the edges of the shield, willing them to grow slowly to extend to where the three of them stood. I knew the moment it had worked when Anthony let out a small whoop of delight behind me, and I tried not to feel cocky. Anything could still go wrong, and the body hadn't been dealt with yet.

Opening my eyes now, I focused on the body on the ground, clicking my fingers and resisting the urge to let out a relieved breath when two small balls of flame appeared, floating above each hand. I could feel the power flowing through me. Seconds later, though, I could feel panic kick in when the flames began to dance before me, the fire growing quickly, unlike when I'd used my abilities in front of the Order the week before. The flames grew so large that I could feel what little control I had slipping away further, almost like my magic had a mind of its own.

"What the fuck..." Anthony said loudly, and Anika shushed him.

Liam stepped close behind me, his chest pressing against my back while he ran his fingers slowly along my arms before cupping my hands with his.

"Just lean into me, Isolde. Use my power to control yours." He whispered in my ear, and the magic began stabilising. The balls of fire were again controlled, and I relaxed a little into Liam's arms. I remembered now that when I'd used my ability at the Manor, Liam's hand had been on my shoulder, and I wondered if that had been the real reason I'd been able to control the flame then.

Both balls of fire were huge now but no longer flickering erratically, and we raised our arms together, merging the flames before us. I inhaled deeply while we guided the ball toward the body and watched it erupt into flames. Nightwalker bodies combusted when set alight, and this one was no different.

"Oh shit!" Anthony suddenly remembered the head still in his hand and threw it into the flames before they disappeared, and I laughed. I never thought I would find death and destruction funny, but there was something so hilarious about watching the head fly through the air, and I wondered if maybe I'd just hit the final point of my sanity and was now completely unhinged. But Anika and Liam also huffed out a laugh, and that made me feel better. At least I wasn't alone in the madness.

Anika and Anthony stepped up beside us, staring silently down at where the body had previously been. All that remained was a scorched patch of grass, with small puffs of smoke drifting upwards.

"That was..." Anika seemed to be searching for the right words.

"Fucking brilliant." Anthony was grinning while he finished her sentence. He looked like a kid who had just unwrapped a shiny new toy at Christmas, although Anika looked slightly more unsure. She looked at Liam.

"Have you always been able to do that?"

I felt Liam shake his head, his hands still cupping mine.

"No, I seem to be able to tap into Isolde's power, but that was mostly her. I just felt the pull towards her then to help her control it."

I turned my hands over and laced my fingers through his, squeezing them while I lowered them to my side.

"Let's go. I wanna see that again!" Anthony was bouncing on his feet. Anika looked at us for a beat longer before nodding, following him out of the bushes. Liam pulled me back when I moved to follow them, turning me to face him before crushing his mouth to mine. He ran his hands into my hair, holding me tight against him and kissing me hungrily.

"I forgot how great that feels," He said, his lips still pressed to mine. I nodded, still feeling the power crackle through us both. The few times he had previously channelled my magic, we'd immediately climbed all over each other. Still, I wasn't interested in having an audience, so we had to make do with another brief kiss. Pulling away reluctantly, I looked up at him, ensuring he knew we would pick this up once we were alone, before following our companions out of the bushes and hunting down another nightwalker to set on fire.

After taking out four more nightwalkers, we returned to the house shortly before dawn. It was the most I'd ever come across in a single night when there wasn't a nest involved, which was both exciting and terrifying. I'd remained relatively quiet on the walk back to the house, not feeling the need to join Anika and Anthony as they ran back in a blur. Liam remained silent at my side, allowing me to mull over my thoughts without interference. It wasn't until we reached our room that I finally started asking the questions forming in my mind.

"Why aren't the Order out there, focussing on where the real problems are? Surely they are aware of the risk posed to those sleeping rough?"

"Honestly, I think it's because they are more focused on keeping the presence of vampires a secret."

I could see my concern mirrored in his eyes, which was a bit of a relief.

"Did you never patrol with them in the past? Surely you understood this world better than the Order?" I was struggling to wrap my head around all of this. Liam ran his hand through his hair as he shrugged his shoulders.

"Although I've sometimes been in the houses that Eve inhabited, it was never longer than a few weeks, and I never went out on patrol. What they have all said is true. I spent more time with the Order, attempting to maintain my hold on the human aspect of myself. I've been so focused on my resentment of Eve that I've avoided them all, yet in one day of being with them alongside you, I'm beginning to realise just how little I was aware of." He had moved closer to the window and stared outside as if the darkness held the answers he desperately sought.

"I don't know that I'd go that far, Liam. I still don't trust the daywalkers entirely. From what I can tell, they only patrol to keep the nightwalkers from growing any larger in number. I don't think saving humanity is particularly concerning to them." I moved to stand beside him, raising my hand to touch him lightly on the cheek. I didn't like what the last few weeks had done to his confidence, even though, at the same time, I questioned why he had allowed himself to be so led astray by the Order. He turned to face me and put his arms around me, pulling me close to bury his face in my hair, and sighed.

"I think we did the right thing after all in coming here." He murmured into my hair, and I nodded.

"Me too. But I still want to know what Eve's plan is. It surely can't just be that she wants us close, to be part of her big happy family."

"Agreed. I think she knows far more about the prophecy than what she has told us, and I want to know what that is. But for now, let's try and get some sleep." He guided me towards the giant bed where I had lain for a week in the transition phase. I resisted at first, not sure I wanted to return to it. But after hours of tapping into my powers, sleep was calling my name, and I eventually gave in, sinking beside him and allowing him to hold me close while we fell asleep, the first of dawn's rays beginning to show around the edges of the curtains.

"I see you and my brother have had a busy night." Once again, just after sleep claimed me, I stood across the room from Connor, where he sat in the same chair, swirling yet another glass of whiskey in his hand.

"Seriously, Connor, what's the go? Why do you keep pulling me in here? Don't you have other people you can annoy the crap out of?" I returned to my usual place, leaning against the wall furthest from him. I'd stopped being afraid of him at this point, knowing he wouldn't hurt me, although I was still unsure why.

"You're so much more fun to talk to than the rest. And watching your sister screw anyone who looks her way is becoming tiresome. Even dear William is growing bored of her and returning to his previous obsession with you."

I knew he was trying to goad me into a reaction, but I refused to rise to the bait, even though the mention of my sister and former fiance made me feel queasy.

"What's so fun about talking to me, Connor?" I watched his every move, aware that I lay asleep in his brother's arms while this conversation happened in my mind.

"You fascinate me, Isolde. All these years of waiting for you to arrive, can you blame me for wanting to see the woman foretold to bring about the destruction of my kind?"

"How do you have powers? None of the other nightwalkers seem to have magical abilities, yet here we are, having a conversation in our minds only." I had no idea if he would answer me, but I figured I'd give it a shot.

Connor smirked at me.

"You still have so much to learn, little one. I see Eve is still playing her games." He got up and walked towards me.

I watched him warily, refusing to move. He stopped in front of me, standing so close that I could feel his breath on my face when he looked down at me. I stood completely still while he ran a finger over my neck at where he'd bitten me, the wound long since healed.

"Come and find me again once you work it out." He kissed my forehead while the dream dissolved around us again, and I settled into a dreamless sleep.

Chapter Nineteen

T HE NEXT FEW DAYS followed the same pattern as the first. Our days were spent catching up on the few hours of sleep we needed in the mornings, sharing a meal with whoever was around in the afternoons and evenings, and patrolling at night.

I was receiving regular updates from Ainslie about my family and was relieved that, so far, Aurora was keeping her distance. They had decided to tell people that she'd had a psychotic break and was dangerous... I wasn't sure if that would help, but something was better than nothing.

More daywalkers had begun to arrive, and like usual, they were all fascinated by my presence, which was growing old. Eve had been avoiding us for the most part, and I was impressed at her sexual appetite. A seemingly endless stream of daywalkers walking through her bedroom door, a constant rotation of her little band of followers. I'd witnessed this in Liam's memories, but watching it in person was different.

"Is she ever going to tell us what she has planned?" I expressed my frustration to Liam when we walked back into our room after another meal with Anika and Anthony while Eve remained sequestered in her room.

"Eve never does anything without a plan. I have no doubt that this little parade of sex buddies is for our benefit." Liam said, and I could tell he was also over the games.

"Well, it's not working. Other than making me wonder if her lady parts need to be iced."

Liam laughed, turning to pull me towards him.

"Want to give her a run for her money?" He began kissing down my neck, and I leaned into him with a sigh.

"How about we don't worry about competing." I drew his lips to mine, squealing when he reached down and swiftly grabbed the back of my thighs like I weighed nothing, bringing my legs up to wrap around his waist. We continued to kiss hungrily while he pushed me back against the wall, and I allowed all other thoughts to fall from my mind as we explored even more ways to add to the mingled cries that moved through the house.

That evening, we decided to forego patrolling, and once darkness had fallen, I found my way into the library that took up the entire length of the back of the house on the top floor. Liam had gone to get us dinner, and I had downed yet another glass of blood before deciding to settle down with a book. Since everything in my life had exploded, all my reading had been focussed on research, and I was now faced with the daunting task of choosing a book to read for pleasure.

It felt strange to have time out while the world was going to shit, but my anxiety was beginning to spiral, and

I would be useless to anyone if I didn't get my emotions under control.

I ran my fingers along the shelves while I read through the titles along the long wall of shelves. Nothing was jumping out at me, and I wondered if I'd lost the ability to read for enjoyment, along with so much else in my former life.

I was pulled from my musings by the sound of a book falling from the shelf, which made me jump, and I looked over to see a small leather-bound book lying on the floor across the room. There was no one else in the room, and where once this would have freaked me out, I knew without a doubt that someone had used magic to bring this book to my attention. I moved to pick it up, turning it over to read the gold writing embossed on the front. THE PHOENIX PROPHECY.

Oh dear god, not another prophecy book... The last one I read had utterly upended my life, and I wasn't sure I was ready for another one. I cautiously opened the book, worried I'd set off some terrifying chain of events just by lifting the cover. It was only a few pages long, and the paper was delicate.

In a world blemished by darkness and light,
A young woman shall rise with power and might.
Her destiny was foretold in a prophecy of old,
To bring balance to the turmoil untold.
Of seventh son and seventh daughter born,
Her heart will be set to mourn.
There will be trials that she must endure,
Before she reaches the future so pure.
Her power will be unmatched and rare,

Her soul will be pure, her intentions fair.
But to end the apocalypse, she must pay a cost,
To sacrifice what she loves and lost.
A decision she must make with a heavy heart,
For she knows this is where her journey must start.
With tears in her eyes, she'll rise with grace,
To battle the evil she must face.
The fate of the world will rest upon her hand,
As she brings an end to the chaos of the land.
Her journey will end with a triumph so bright,
As she brings balance between the wrong and the right.

The words triggered a memory of my own for a change, and I flashed back to my dream when Connor and Aurora first kidnapped me. The words had floated in front of me, but with everything that had happened since then, I'd forgotten all about it. Unable to move, I read the words so many times that my eyes started to blur, trying to understand the meaning behind the words. None of it sounded good to me, except that I would triumph... Triumph how, though?

Liam entered the room at the door furthest from where I sat, clearing his throat to get my attention.

"You okay?" He asked as I remained staring at the book. He came to stand behind me and peered over my shoulder to read the words that were now swimming on the page before me.

"I don't know, to be honest," I said, looking up at him and watching his eyes move back and forth while he quickly read each line, his eyes growing wider with each word. "Have you never actually read the prophecy before?"

"No one had ever shown me, but I've been told about it. But they'd never told me the exact wording."

"Out of curiosity, what did you know, Liam?" I tried not to sound judgemental, but I could tell my words had hit a sore spot when he winced. "Sorry." I gently placed a hand on his cheek, and he turned to place a kiss on my palm before straightening up.

"We've established that I knew very little about anything." He led the way back into the kitchen, and I followed behind him, clutching the book to my chest. As far as I was concerned, this was my book now. I watched while he plated up our Thai food, taking the plate he handed me before sitting beside me at the breakfast bar.

"I think it's time we sat down with Eve," I said, taking a mouthful of food. Liam grimaced, taking his own bite of food and chewing slowly before answering.

"I know we need to, but I also know how impossible it is to get that woman to talk when she isn't ready. She's got something planned, I can tell."

"So we just wait until she decides we're allowed to know the truth about ourselves?" I was not on board with this plan.

"You've seen how difficult it is to get Eve to give a straight answer at the best of times. You're welcome to try and discuss it with her. If you can pry her away from her line of men." Liam shook his head while he continued eating.

"Not just men. I've also seen a few women head in there," I said, and Liam nodded.

"Very true. She doesn't particularly have a preference." We continued eating in silence whilst I thought this over.

"Does it bother you at all? Did you ever have feelings for her?" I wasn't sure why I was asking, as I was pretty sure I didn't want to know the answer, but I had to accept that he'd spent centuries on this planet before I was conceived, and no matter how he felt about me, I knew that other women had warmed his bed.

Liam scanned my face before answering.

"In the beginning, I was enamoured with her. I didn't see her for about ten years after she turned me, and I was interested in this life enough to spend time with her. But there was never the connection that I craved. I think she's been separated from humanity for so long that she's lost the ability to connect on an emotional level. And that was something that I needed. I didn't understand that until I met you, though." He took my hand in his, and I squeezed his fingers lightly.

"I think from what I've seen, although she doesn't appear to have any connection to humanity in the same sense we do, there is still something there. She wants you. I know that my presence, whilst necessary apparently, grates on her. The looks I've received from her show that she does *not* love having someone else playing with someone that she believes belongs to her."

"If I belong to anyone, Isolde, it's you." His words were sweet, and yet there was something that struck a chord deep within me.

"I don't think you belong to anyone but yourself, Liam. You've been searching for who you are and your place in the world for so long. I hope you know that I see who you truly are?"

He looked at me, and I could tell he was trying to believe me.

"Who am I? Because you're right, I have been searching without realising it for so long. I thought I was a Protector, different from all the other daywalkers, but now I have no idea where I fit in or my purpose in this world." The sadness in his eyes broke my heart, and I touched his face again.

"Only you can answer that, Liam. I can only tell you who you are to me. You have been my protector and source of comfort through so much, but that is who you are to me. I can't be your sole purpose, nor you mine. We need to work out together what both our paths are, regardless of any bloody prophecies. But the positive thing is, I'm not going anywhere. We are stuck together now through it all. Whatever the next step ends up being." I brought my forehead to his, and he closed his eyes, taking a deep breath.

"For someone who has only been walking this earth for such a short time, I sometimes feel like you know far more than me, my love." He kissed my forehead, and it was my turn to take a deep breath, pushing aside the feeling of deja vu that hit me at the action. It was so close to what Connor had done during our last interaction. The less I compared the two of them, the better. That way would only lead to more pain and confusion, and I wasn't ready to deal with any of that yet. I wasn't sure that I would ever be.

Chapter Twenty

"*U*GH. DOESN'T IT GET *tiring being so sickening-ly in love and stroking each other's egos all the time?*"

Once again, Conor pulled me into the mindscape, and we were in our usual positions. In the real world, Liam and I were wrapped around each other, having fallen asleep after another round of lovemaking in our room. By now, I could tell Connor seemed to have access to my movements in the real world, and I didn't bother hiding my sneer.

"*There's that jealousy again, Connor,*" *I said, my arms crossed while I watched him throw back yet another glass of whiskey.*

"*Hardly. The two of you exhaust me. All of those pesky feelings and insecurities flying around is enough to drive me to drink.*" *He poured himself another drink before getting a second glass and pouring another one. He walked towards me and held the glass out towards me.* "*Have a drink with me, Isolde.*"

I hesitated, eyeing the glass in his outstretched hand.

"You watched me pour it. It's not going to hurt you. And besides, it's a fucking dream. Just take the damn drink."

I glared at him before snatching it from his hand, throwing my head back and allowing the whiskey to burn down my throat.

"Good girl."

I scowled at him while I slammed the glass down. It made a satisfying bang when it met the wooden surface.

"I'm not your good girl, Connor." I refused to play into whatever fantasy he was building up in his mind about us being together, even though his presence now confused my brain. I blamed the dream whiskey for how my body seemed drawn towards him when he stood before me. I watched him throw back his drink, clenching my jaw when my traitorous body reacted at the sight of his throat bobbing while he swallowed.

"You're not Liam," I said once again, as a reminder to myself, but knowing it would piss him off.

"How often do I have to remind you I am far more fun than him?" Connor tossed his glass aside, and it smashed against the wall. He stepped closer to me, holding my gaze while he lifted a lock of my hair and twirled it with his finger.

What was it with these men and my hair?

I was cursing the part of me that was unwilling to fight the control he seemed to have over me, unable to step away even while he gathered my hair around his fist and tipped my head back slightly, forcing my gaze to meet his intense stare.

"What do you want, Connor?" I breathed out a sigh when he lowered his forehead to mine. Why couldn't I control my body around this man? I knew he was evil and

meant to be my mortal enemy, and yet I was drawn to him like a fucking moth to a flame. I lowered my gaze to his lips, and he chuckled, aware of my every movement.

"Seems like my baby brother might not be enough for you, little one." He grazed his lips over mine before stepping back with what looked like immense effort, and I felt the loss of his presence, even though I could breathe a little easier now that he was further away.

"He is more than enough for me. I still maintain that you are doing something to me. I love Liam. I hate you." I glared at him, and he smirked, raking a hand through his hair while his eyes flashed again. "And why the fuck do your eyes keep doing that?"

He raised an eyebrow.

"I think the question you're asking is why have your eyes been doing that?" He stepped closer again and lifted my chin to gaze into my eyes. "You're starting to realise that there are so many differences between yourself and the other daywalkers. Between us and all the other vampires."

I was once again fighting the urge to kiss him and was proud of myself for placing my hand on his chest and pushing him away.

He moved back without resistance, laughing. He was enjoying this far too much.

I was growing more and more annoyed with every moment that passed between us.

"I'm waking up now." I attempted to pull myself out of the connection, but nothing happened, and Connor just watched me with a smirk. "Let me go, Connor."

"But I enjoy talking to you so much more than the others. Let me show you what I'm dealing with right now." The room dissolved around us, and we no longer stood in that

god-forsaken house. I had no idea where he had brought me, but judging by the large room we were standing in, it was yet another massive house. In all my twenty-five years before becoming aware of this world, I had never set foot in homes this fancy. These magical and immortal beings loved to surround themselves with wealth.

But it wasn't the room that held my attention. My eyes were drawn to the couple in the corner who were devouring each other. Aurora ground herself against Will, who lay back on a chaise lounge, surrounded by other nightwalkers. Some were partaking in their own sexual experiences, but a few others watched them hungrily. I felt ill at the sight when Connor stepped close behind me and waved his hand around the room, pointing towards the others.

Connor had brought me to see a vampire orgy, and my sister and former fiance appeared to be the stars of the show.

"Was your sister this much of an exhibitionist in her former life? Because she fucking loves being watched while she's being fucked, and it is growing exhausting watching her ride every member of this coven. She's particularly enamoured with dear William, but I don't think there is anyone left that she hasn't screwed, male or female." Connor ran his hands down my sides while pressing against my back.

I pushed out of his grasp and looked away. I couldn't stomach the look on Aurora's face while she rode Will, staring over his head at the couple standing behind him. The woman ran her hand through my sister's hair.

"Does that mean you've fucked her as well?" I spat the words out as I stormed from the room.

I wanted out of this hellscape now.

Once again, the room around us changed, and we were back in the house. I didn't think I'd ever be grateful to be back here, but anything was better than that. I marched towards the bottle of whiskey and grabbed it by the neck, taking a large drink and slamming it back down, willing the burn to erase the scene from my mind.

"Now who's jealous, Isolde? Don't you like the idea of me buried deep inside your twin sister, fucking her brains out?" He came right after me, grabbing my arm and swinging me around to face him. The smirk on his face was laced with desire, and his chest rose and fell rapidly when he closed the small distance between us. I held myself perfectly still, glaring at him while he held my gaze, gripping my chin to keep me from looking away.

"Yes, you're jealous. You want me, and you hate yourself for it. But you crave my lips on yours." He crushed his mouth to mine, pulling me into his arms and kissing me hungrily before I could react. "You want me to make you scream." His voice was husky while he ran his hands down my sides and yanked my hips into his, forcing me to feel how hard he was against my abdomen. He nipped at my neck between hungry kisses, and I gasped, torn between desire and repulsion at how my body reacted.

"No, I don't." My body was not agreeing with the words coming out of my mouth.

Connor laughed darkly and spun me around, pulling my back flush against his chest while his hands roamed my body. My mind was at war with my body, and I gasped when his lips blazed a path up my neck, stopping at my earlobe, which he took gently between his teeth.

"No, Isolde. You clearly don't want this. You really don't want my hand here," he whispered in my ear while he cupped my breast with his hand, and I arched into his touch.

"And you obviously don't want me to touch you here."
He ran his other hand down my abdomen, and my
breathing quickened when he traced a circle around my
belly button.

"I... don't... want..." I struggled to form words while
his hand moved further south, and I gasped when his fin-
gers slipped beneath the band of my yoga pants, inching
closer and closer to where I was aching between my legs.

"No. You don't want me to make you come over and
over, do you, Isolde?" He began to rub his finger over my
sensitive bud, and I groaned. He moved his hand faster,
feeling my body tense up while he kissed my neck. My hips
began moving of their own accord, and I rode his hand.

"But you shouldn't come, Isolde..."

Just when I was sure my body was about to explode, he
ripped his hands away, whispering in my ear while the
dream faded.

"Because I'm not Liam."

In reality, I sat up quickly, still panting, and nausea
ripped through me. I could feel the sweat covering my
body, causing me to feel cold even in the summer heat.

That fucking asshole.

I leapt from the bed and ran into the bathroom connected to our room, hearing Liam stir when I began
throwing up. He flew into the room behind me and
pulled my hair back out of my face while I retched,
rubbing a soothing hand up and down my back. I had
been unsure if vampires could throw up, but I was
proving it was possible.

Eventually, the retching subsided, and I reached up to
flush the toilet before leaning back against the cabinet as I

sat on the cold tiles. Liam poured me a glass of water and pressed it into my hands, urging me to drink.

"Are you okay?" He slid down to sit beside me and put an arm around me. I realised I was shaking and fought not to throw up again at the memory of his brother's hands all over me.

"Yeah." I let my head fall to his shoulder and stared at the wall opposite where we sat.

"What happened?" There was no suspicion in Liam's voice, and his complete trust in me felt like a knife was being driven into my heart. I decided to go with a bit of the truth.

"Connor pulled me into his mind again and showed me Aurora screwing the entire coven."

Liam's grip on me tightened, pulling me in closer.

"I'm so sorry, Isolde. I wish I knew how to break his hold over your mind. I'll talk to Eve and see if we can do anything. Maybe the Order knows a spell." I felt his jaw clench against my forehead where I was leaning into his chest, and I nodded.

I had a feeling there was no way to break this. And a small part of me wondered if I even wanted to. Because aside from being forced to watch my sister grind against the former love of my life, a small, treacherous part of me wished Connor had finished what he'd started.

And I hated myself for that.

Chapter Twenty-One

T HE FOLLOWING DAY, I got up earlier than Liam, unable to sleep properly after the interaction with Connor. Although daywalkers didn't require much sleep, I was pretty sure we needed more than what I'd had last night.

I was exhausted and pissed off.

Very pissed off.

I was done with having no control over these inter-actions with Connor and my sleeping mind being easily seduced by his crap. I chose to ignore that my waking brain was also confused.

I loved Liam. That was all I was focussing on right now. And Liam deserved better than a girlfriend who was horny for his literal evil twin.

I stumbled into the kitchen, intent on making a giant cup of coffee. Anika was already there, making herself some breakfast. It was so rare to see her without Anthony that I stopped still for a moment, unsure what to do. She smiled over at me, perhaps sensing my confusion.

"Anthony is having a lie-in. But I've never been great at lying around once I'm awake. You can join me if you want?"

Of all the other daywalkers in this house, Anika and Anthony were the only ones who made me feel even slightly welcome. The rest either acted like we didn't exist or watched me warily. We were still waiting to learn how this prophecy was meant to play out and what the whole "she will end the war" part truly meant.

"Thanks. I'd like that," I said, and I was surprised that I meant that. Anika was such a ray of sunshine amongst all of these crabby daywalkers. If it weren't for her, I wasn't sure Anthony would be half as nice as he was. He was only just bearable as it was, constantly throwing sarcastic comments our way and trying to get under Liam's skin. I think seeing us in action had earned his begrudging admiration, but even so, he liked to make pointed remarks about the Order at any chance he could. Liam took it reasonably well, but we had been avoiding too much time around him unless we were patrolling together. He at least respected our abilities and rarely said anything rude when we were setting bodies on fire.

I accepted the bowl of fruit Anika handed me, and we sat at one of the tables near the window. A part of the kitchen had been set up with cafe-style tables and chairs, allowing the option to sit in smaller groups or join others at one of the more oversized tables on the deck.

"I thought I heard you up through the night. No offence, but you look awful." Anika commented before she took a mouthful of food, and I grimaced, taking my own bite before answering.

"It would appear that Liam's brother had set up some psychic connection between us when he attempted to turn me. So he's been taking liberties and entering my dreams unannounced to fuck with me."

Anika paused, her spoon halfway to her mouth as she processed what I said.

"Wait, a nightwalker has psychic abilities? How is that possible?" Her spoon clattered back down to her bowl.

"No idea. Liam seems to think it was because Connor had abilities before he was turned, but that doesn't track with everything we know, right? From what I've been told, Order members have transitioned in the past, and their abilities didn't remain. Honestly, there is so much about Connor that doesn't track with anything I know about nightwalkers. He seems different to the others." I wasn't sure why I was relaying my concerns to Anika, someone I barely knew. Still, I realised that the list of people I could confide in was minimal these days, and Liam wasn't great about discussing anything to do with his brother and his connection with me.

"I've never had the pleasure of meeting Connor, but I've heard the stories. He's one of the worst amongst them, Isolde. Don't let whatever shit he's twisting around up there fool you." She gestured towards my head. "They are all predators, and it sounds like he's toying with his food."

"Oh, I believe you. He's a bastard. He took great pleasure in showing me what my sister and... Actually, you know what, I don't want to talk about that anymore. I don't feel like throwing up again." I slid the bowl away from me, unable to continue eating. Just the thought of seeing Aurora and Will take part in that depraved vampire orgy was enough to turn me off my food.

Anika watched me while she continued eating.

"You know, we've been waiting for the chosen one to come along for a long time, but I don't think anyone ever considered how crap it would be for you. I'm guessing that's also the case within the Order?"

I nodded, and Anika clucked her tongue and screwed up her face.

"Did you know about the Gemini Prophecy as well?" I asked.

Anika shrugged before answering.

"Some of it. I wasn't aware of Liam's involvement. I always put Eve's interest in him down to the fact that she wasn't used to not getting her way. It's been amusing watching him get the upper hand with her over the years."

I tried to smile but didn't enjoy being reminded of Liam's past with Eve. Even though I knew how much she annoyed the crap out of him.

Anika reached across the table and squeezed my hand.

"I know it seems like it, but not all daywalkers are completely devoid of human feelings like the Order would have you believe."

"In my own limited experience, aside from yourself and occasionally Anthony, that has been the case," I said pointedly, and Anika laughed.

"True, most of the ones you've met here haven't been great, but they are all Eve's little lackeys. Liam has spent most of his years avoiding daywalker interactions, but a few have remained quite human. They seem to be the ones who have managed to forge an actual emotional attachment to someone. There is a lot about this world that neither of you understand. Being forced to see the truth behind the Order will be great for you both."

I thought about what she said for a moment.

"I have a question. If it's not rude to ask?" I asked, and Anika nodded.

"Ask away. I'm an open book."

I believed her, too.

"Liam mentioned that he'd met a daywalker couple once who were bonded. Like we were before I transitioned. Is that you and Anthony? I've watched how the two of you move around each other when no one else is around, and it's almost as though you can read each other's thoughts?"

Anika smiled.

"You're very observant. Many others hadn't picked up on that, but with his abilities, Liam picked it right away, of course."

"Our bond hasn't survived the transition, but Liam said you were bonded before your transition. Was there any time when you couldn't hear each other?" I was clutching at straws, hoping that the bond would return and she might have the answers.

She sat back, quiet for a moment before answering.

"I met Anthony when I was a member of the Order, and he had already become a daywalker."

I felt my eyebrows rise, and Anika laughed. That was the furthest from my mind of everything I thought she might say.

"That's right. I knew Liam when I was a human, although we didn't live in the same group. I was in the New York Manor. I had only just learned about this world and was quite young within the Order when I met Anthony on patrol one night. He was intrigued by me, and I him. You know how the Order feels about daywalkers, obviously. So I met him often in secret, and we eventually fell in love. It wasn't long after he first fed off me that the bond formed. I still don't understand what happened, but I suspect my magical abilities did it. I was one of the Order members with psychic abilities, like yourself and Liam, so I think that is part of the reason. But I never had the chance to investigate it further. For obvious reasons, I couldn't tell anyone in the Order about it, and Liam only found out after I became a daywalker." Anika shrugged, seeming content to leave the story there, but I still had many questions. I was unaware that other Order members had become daywalkers other than Liam. There was still so much I didn't know, which was frustrating.

"So your bond survived the transition entirely, then? You didn't have any issues when you first turned?" I was desperate to know if there was any chance of the bond between myself and Liam reforming.

Anika shook her head, and I deflated a little.

"No, we never had a time where the bond was broken. I wish I had that answer for you."

The sadness must have been showing on my face because she reached across the table and squeezed my hand again.

"I keep wondering if I've come through the transition broken...." I hadn't voiced this concern to myself, let alone to anyone else, and saying it now made me feel like crying. I could already feel the tears forming in the corners of my eyes.

Anika got up and pulled her seat around to sit next to me, wrapping her arm around me and giving me a side hug. I was taken aback at such a comforting gesture, and I froze for a moment before allowing her to provide me with what support she could. Since I'd transitioned, aside from the brief interaction with my parents and sisters, I'd had no physical touch from anyone other than Liam, and I realised now how much I needed it.

"I don't think you're broken, Isolde. I think that you've had to deal with a lot, and it's going to take time to work out who you are now," Anika said.

I felt a tear escape, making its way down my cheek.

"It also probably doesn't help that you've got a psychotic asshole whispering to you in your sleep."

I laughed, but it came out as a snort, and we both cracked up laughing – a nice bit of humour amongst all the sadness.

Anika moved her seat back to sit across from me again, and I sat back in my chair, studying her.

"So, you were in the Order? Do they know that you're a daywalker now?"

Anika nodded, a twinkle in her eye.

"Oh, they know. There have actually been a few of us over the years. But I'm guessing they didn't tell you that. I think we're a bit of a dirty little secret amongst the elders. Those of us who chose this life over remaining in the Order aren't something they want widely known. When I transitioned, the head of the New York Manor was not impressed. The fact that they allowed Liam to remain amongst them has always made the rest of us quite curious about why... But now that we know the truth of the prophecy, it makes sense. They wanted to control him."

"So is that why Anthony gives Liam such a hard time about remaining with the Order? Because of how they treated you?" I wondered at what point Anika would grow tired of my questions, but it felt good to have someone who gave me straight answers.

"Well, most daywalkers have a pretty low opinion of the members of the Order. But yeah, he wasn't impressed with how quickly my supposed family cast me aside, especially because I turned to avoid death altogether. I didn't go to Anthony and ask him to change me. I was fighting with a nightwalker and thrown off a bridge. The fact that I didn't die immediately was a miracle, but Anthony was with me, and I would have died if he hadn't turned me. We were already in love, and the idea of continuing to live without me wasn't something he could handle. I imagine Liam was presented with the same issue when he turned you?" She asked.

"To a degree. I'd made him promise that if there were ever a chance I might return as a nightwalker to ensure that didn't happen. I know he hoped it would never come to that, but it turns out it was always our destiny for him to turn me into a daywalker." I wondered if the bitterness I felt at what we'd been forced into would ever dissipate.

"I know your psychic bond may not have survived the transition, but I can promise you one thing. The love that you have for one another is still there. I don't have Liam's ability to read people's minds, but I've seen how you both are together. You are each other's strength, and I think that is more important than any other bond that exists. Hold onto each other, Isolde. Love like that doesn't come along every day. I get the feeling that what is coming will be particularly difficult. I can sense the change, and I know you have too."

I tried not to shiver at her words, but I knew she was right, and I wondered how long it would be before we were forced to face whatever had been unleashed on the world the night Liam was forced to turn me.

And I wondered if we would be ready.

Chapter Twenty-Two

THAT NIGHT, LIAM AND I headed out to patrol once again. This time, we decided to go solo, figuring we could cover more ground if we spread out from the others. And Liam was pissed at Anthony, who had had another dig at him earlier in the day. I hadn't been there, but I'd heard the two of them arguing, and when I'd asked what had happened, Liam had just said not to worry about it. I figured it was probably something to do with the Order, so I let it be.

We'd decided to hit Roma Street Parklands, and not long after midnight, I trailed behind Liam when he led the way along the darkened path amongst the gardens. We'd been here a few nights earlier and noticed more nightwalkers lurking nearby. I was growing very concerned at the alarming number of nightwalkers we were finding and realised that the Order honestly had no idea how many people were being turned.

I was shaken from my dark thoughts when I noticed a movement out of the corner of my eye, and I managed to alert Liam by calling his name before the nightwalker hidden amongst the trees flung itself at him. My ability to sense them in the dark was on high alert, and I knew there were more nearby. I moved forward to assist Liam but was ripped backwards by a second nightwalker and turned to face my attacker. In life, the girl in front of me would have been lucky to have been around seventeen. I pushed that thought aside while I moved to strike her in the chest with my fist. She flew backwards and hit a tree with a grunt, though it barely seemed to stun her before she rushed towards me again.

I could still hear Liam fighting with the other nightwalker, leaving me to continue fighting against her alone. She drew close again, and I leapt into the air, striking her with my foot. She flew back again, landing in a heap on the ground. I moved quickly, tapping into my new vampire speed, and was on top of her before she could rise again. I still wasn't sure I could handle killing a nightwalker with Anthony's preferred method of ripping their heads from their shoulders, so I settled for driving my stake into her heart, moving before she'd even had a chance to blink up at me.

Liam's opponent was more mature than the vampire I'd taken on, and he was giving Liam a bit of a harder time than the one I'd just killed. I rose to assist him while the nightwalker squared off against him. Watching Liam fight constantly reminded me of watching a well-choreographed dance, and it was no different now. He circled the male, skilfully avoiding each punch he unleashed. Reading your opponent's mind was a convenient skill, and I smirked when Liam sidestepped a kick that would have caused great pain to a human. I could tell that Liam had the upper hand, so I just settled myself to watch. I knew it was probably twisted to be turned on by watching your lover in a fight to the death, but it was hard not to be aroused as Liam's muscles rippled with each movement while he played with the nightwalker. Perhaps Liam was using him to burn off some lingering frustrations he felt with being around Eve and her brethren.

Finally deciding to put the creature out of his misery, Liam made a similar move to the one I had earlier, unleashing a kick that sent it flying backwards. I heard its spine snap as it smacked hard into the tree behind him. But a snapped spine wasn't enough to stop a nightwalker. Liam was upon it immediately. He slammed his stake into its chest, watching with a dangerous smile while the light dimmed from its startling blue eyes. He rose slowly before turning to face me while I watched him closely.

"Feel better?" I asked, resisting the urge to move closer and climb him. The spark in Liam's eye told me he had an inkling of where my thoughts had gone, and he smirked a little. He would have started strutting if he was any other man, but Liam didn't need to strut. He was confident enough to know just how good he was.

"A little. We should probably get rid of these before we keep going?" He gestured towards the bodies, and I nodded.

He dragged the body of the vampire he'd killed over to where my former opponent lay before moving towards me. A slight shiver ran through me when he stopped behind me, running both hands down my sides, pressing his chest against my back and covering my hands with his own. Even without raising our hands, I could feel the connection between us grow, and I took a steadying breath while I pushed my arousal aside, trying to concentrate on raising the barrier around us. I felt a rumble in his chest when he chuckled, and I knew he could feel my emotions through the magic that rippled around us.

"You are not helping," I said quietly, and he kissed my neck.

"Sorry." He didn't sound even remotely sorry, but I managed to get myself under control, feeling the power run through us both. I laced my fingers through his, raising his arms with mine.

"Hide and protect us," I whispered, and the air around us began to crackle once again when the barrier raised around us, cloaking us from prying eyes. I willed the flame into being before guiding it towards the bodies, watching with satisfaction when they erupted in flames. Each time we performed the magic together, it became easier. If any members of the Order were to witness this, they would be terrified at the power we could wield together. I knew it could be dangerous and that it could be hard not to get caught up in that power. To become lost in it and set the world ablaze. The flames remained unstable when I channelled them on my own, and I worried that if I were to test it without Liam, it would burn out of control. I could feel Liam tighten his grip on my hands while we worked together to keep the fire under control as the bodies exploded.

Once all traces were gone, I extinguished the flame, and we breathed a collective sigh, the magic still rolling through us both. I could feel the barrier around us continuing to crackle, and I turned slowly in his arms, reaching to loop my arms around his neck when he pulled me in close and lowered his lips to mine. We kissed hungrily, and I was grateful we'd decided to patrol without the others tonight. It had been hard to resist the pull towards each other when we'd patrolled with Anika and Anthony, but with the barrier around us and no one else within its confines, there was no need to deny ourselves tonight.

"I need you," I whispered against his lips, and he groaned, nodding his head while he trailed kisses down my neck. His hands moved their way down to grip my hips. We worked together to remove my leggings before he pushed me back against the tree that was thankfully within the barrier with us. I was already ready for him, and he was buried inside me within seconds, having freed himself of his belt and undoing his jeans. We sighed together when he moved his hips slowly, my legs wrapped tight around his waist, and my head fell back against the tree, giving him access to my throat. He kissed me hungrily before biting down, and I moaned while the pleasure shot through me. His bite alone was enough to take me over the edge, and I cried out when the orgasm rocked through me. He continued to move at a leisurely pace, and I managed to find the sweet spot that allowed him to press against where I needed him most with each movement. He moved his mouth away from my neck and pressed his forehead against mine, our eyes locked while we continued to move together. Feeling his orgasm growing, I pressed my mouth to his neck, knowing that my bite would have the same intense reaction for him. He moaned when I bit down, my teeth growing sharper, and we both found our release while his blood made its way down my throat.

I pulled my mouth back when he slowed his movements against me. We brought our foreheads together again, closing our eyes while the magic continued to flow and the pleasure rolled through us both in waves.

"God, that's addictive," Liam whispered, holding me close.

We were both shaking, and it took a few minutes before I could lower my legs to the ground and support myself while he grabbed my leggings, helping me pull them back on. Somehow, the barrier was still up, and after a few more minutes of holding each other close, we brought it down together, stepping back onto the path and heading off in search of more nightwalkers.

Chasing the rush of the magic and the pleasure that still rocketed through us both.

Two hours and several stabbing and sex sessions later, we decided to call it a night. The adrenaline from all the fighting, magic and fucking made me jittery, and I could tell Liam was feeling the same.

Perhaps we should try not to succumb to the crazed urge to go at it each time. I feel like my heart is about to beat out of my chest. I thought to myself while we walked over the footbridge between the gardens and South Bank.

I looked over at Liam, who nodded as though I'd said the words out loud.

I stared at him when he looked over at where I'd come to a sudden halt in the middle of the bridge.

Why'd she stop? Liam looked around us.

I knew the moment he picked up on my racing thoughts when his eyes snapped back to mine.

Can you hear me? His gaze was intense while he searched my face.

Yes.

I was torn between euphoria and terror, and I knew my head was an incoherent mess, even while he pulled me hard against him and hugged me tightly. I couldn't tell if my heart was racing due to the continued adrenaline or the realisation that our bond had finally returned.

It must have been all the magic we were using tonight. Liam's voice in my head was filled with joy at the knowledge that he could hear my thoughts again. However, the joy faded when he sensed I wasn't as delighted as he was. *What's wrong?*

"I don't know that you're ready to handle how messed up my head is now," I answered out loud. I searched his face, and his expression softened.

I remember how hard it was in the beginning. At least now I can help you sort through the mess. And I can help keep Connor out now.

I refused to let my mind wander to thoughts of Connor right now. No matter what he thought, he was not ready to see what his brother was capable of.

I allowed him to hold me close and pushed all thoughts except my love for him out of my head, determined not to allow this moment to be ruined by evil twins and potentially fucked up girlfriends.

Chapter Twenty-Three

WE ARRIVED BACK AT the house and headed straight for the shower. Because our bond had only truly formed the day before I was turned, we'd never had the opportunity to explore its full potential. And by full potential, I meant during sex. Liam had always been able to hear me when we'd been together while I was a human, but hearing his thoughts while he was buried inside me and had me pressed against the shower wall was a new and addictive experience. But after the night we'd had of giving in to our animalistic needs over and over, we were both exhausted and passed out as soon as we crawled into bed.

This time, instead of being pulled into Connor's mind, a memory began to form the moment my eyes drifted closed.

I entered the large auditorium, intent on getting a glimpse of her. I'd felt the change in the air for months and knew that it meant that the female twins were now activated. They must have turned twenty-five in January, the younger one coming into her powers and about to become part of the aggravating Order of the Dragon. It had taken me this long to find out who she was, and now I knew where she would be with the aid of one of Adam's latest recruits. The internet was still a bit of a mystery to those of us who had been around long enough to remember a time before modern technology ruled the world, so he'd turned a cyber expert a few months ago, and it was proving quite handy. However, said expert spent more time ripping people apart than sitting in front of a computer, which wasn't ideal. I had long grown tired of cleaning up the messes left behind by all the damn young ones Adam was turning left, right and centre. He was paranoid now that we knew the 'Chosen One' was active. He still knew nothing about the Gemini Prophecy, though. I doubted I would have survived this long if he had any inkling of the true power I wielded. How I had managed to keep it from him for all these years felt like a miracle, but I suspected there was more behind it than that, like so much else in my god-forsaken existence. I needed to find a way to bring it to his attention soon, though.

Adam had been trying to get to her for the last few weeks, but Liam was always lurking in the dark, playing the part of a good little protector. I knew they were waiting for her tattoo to form fully. It never ceased to amaze me at how stu-pid they were, letting their newest members walk around, clueless, until their tattoos were fully formed. They were usually sitting ducks if we got wind of any of them first. But not this one. The protection surrounding her was fucking ridiculous. But they thought she was safe during the day. And I loved the challenge.

I looked around while I moved towards the stairs leading to the back of the lecture theatre. I felt her eyes on me before I could locate her, but once my gaze met hers, I knew it was her instantly. I would have known this was her even if I hadn't seen her social media profiles. It was like she was calling me to her. And I was fucking hooked.

She was gorgeous, even casually dressed, with her long, dark hair tied in a messy bun. And to think, there was another woman as identically stunning out there. How did their poor little human men manage to stand tall in front of such beauties and think they were equal? That boyfriend was a lucky man. Or should I say fiance now, judging by the massive rock on her finger? Good luck actually making it down the aisle.

She watched me intently while I made my way to the back of the room, turning fully in her seat to keep her eyes locked on mine. I wondered if she'd ever seen Liam and was mistaking me for him. The thought aggravated me. I was tired of being reminded that my saintly brother was out there. We'd come face to face a few times over the centuries, and each time, it was a punch to the gut.

She finally realised she was staring at me and blushed before turning back around, busying herself with preparing for the class. I kept my eyes on her the entire time. From how she sat, I knew she was aware of my gaze.

I'd been lurking in shadows for so long I'd forgotten how to be around others and only became aware of how much of a creep I probably looked like to the others around me when the woman next to me cleared her throat loudly. I slowly turned my gaze to hers, and she shrank back in her seat before gathering her belongings and moving a few seats away.

Smart move.

When the lecture drew to a close, I waited until a few of those around me had risen to their feet. Locking onto their minds, I erased any thoughts of my presence and slipped into the shadows once more, moving at speed to leave the room. I'd long ago mastered the ability to disappear. But her presence would remain with me. There was so much connecting us now, and the path we were walking together just became much more interesting...

The memory started to fade around me.

"Interesting." Connor's voice rang out, and I was yanked from his memory into that same room. He wasn't sitting in his usual chair, and I stepped back against the wall, startled by how close he stood before me, looking at me as though trying to peer into my mind.

"What's interesting?" My voice shook slightly, still thrown by the feelings his memory stirred up. I'd had brief glimpses of his mind when I'd seen his interactions with Liam in the blood memories, but this was different.

"I can sense the change in you. Something has finally broken through that barrier you'd thrown up around your mind." He paused momentarily, and his eyes flashed from blue to dark brown and back. Like Liam had described mine doing. I watched him closely, and his face settled into a scowl.

"My god, you're as bad as your fucking twin. Mind you, I didn't realise Liam had it in him to go at it like that all night. Good for him." He glared at me, and I rolled my eyes at his jealousy.

"Wow, getting slut shamed by an evil vampire. Although it doesn't surprise me that you're cheering on the male in the scenario. For someone who frequently tries to get into my pants, you are certainly judgemental... Or do you wish that

it was you I had been riding all night, Connor?" I could tell from his reaction that I'd hit the nail on the head, and I smirked when he stepped back, his eyes flashing again.

"Don't be ridiculous. No point in being jealous when I know I could have you screaming like that half the time." He walked over to the whiskey and poured himself a glass. The man sure did love his whiskey.

"Just keep telling yourself that, Connor. And what do you mean, the barrier I'd thrown up around my mind?"

He threw back the whiskey and placed the glass on the table before moving to sit in the chair again, watching me closely. I remained where I stood, ensuring to keep a distance between us. I didn't need a repeat of what had happened the night before.

"You have no idea of your true powers, do you, little one?" Connor smirked again, and I glowered at him.

"Enough with the cryptic bullshit, Connor," I snapped, and he sighed, shaking his head.

"Dear, dear Isolde. When will you learn how much I love playing with your beautiful mind? Amongst other parts of you." He laughed when I let out a frustrated growl. "And you make it so easy! As if I'm going to give up the answers without having fun first. It's like you know nothing about me at all."

"I don't know anything about you other than this persona you put on for me and the fact that everyone keeps telling me how evil you are," I said, glaring at him.

"Oh, I am evil. Listen to what everyone is telling you, Isolde. They're right about me." His eyes flashed, and he moved so fast that he stopped before me once again before I even had a chance to blink. "I've done so many awful things

you couldn't even imagine," he whispered, and I shivered involuntarily.

"And yet, the glimpses I've had inside your mind tell me that you're not as evil as you want everyone to believe."

He stepped back and looked at me.

"What glimpses inside of my head?"

For once, it seemed he didn't have all the answers.

"The flashes of your memories I've had. Although your memories aren't as strong as Liam's and Aurora's, I've seen some of yours too." His eyes flashed again.

"That's not possible."

"Why not?" I was intrigued that I seemed to have touched on a nerve. He didn't want me inside his head any more than I wanted him inside mine.

"Because I made sure you weren't able to see them." He glared at me like it was somehow my fault.

"Well, I guess you're not as all-powerful as you think, Connor. Cause I've seen through you, and I know you're not the big bad you make yourself out to be." He closed the distance between us again and pressed me back against the wall. His jaw clenched as he placed both hands on the wall on either side of my head.

"Don't talk about things you don't understand, little one." His words were threatening, but I just held his gaze.

"What are you going to do to stop me?"

I was taunting him now, and he knew it. His eyes flashed yet again. I'd never seen him come so close to losing control before, and I could see the cracks starting to show.

"You've had every opportunity to hurt me, yet here we are."

"Do you want me to hurt you, Isolde?" His face was so close to mine that kissing him right now would be so easy, and I *could tell he was thinking about it when his gaze drifted to my lips.*

"No. I'm not into pain."

"I think you might be. I think you'd be begging me to hurt you."

"What. The. Fuck."

Connor spun around, and we both stared at Liam, who was standing in the middle of the room, watching us. The expression on his face made my stomach drop.

"Liam," I said quietly. I shoved Connor out of the way, moving towards Liam, who was glaring at Connor. Once I was within reach, Liam pulled me behind him. I could feel him shaking.

"Brother." Connor tilted his head in mock greeting towards Liam, and Liam erupted. He raced towards his brother, but Connor vanished, and the room dissolved around us.

I sat up straight in bed, and Liam leapt up to get away from me.

"What the fuck Isolde?" He grabbed his shirt and yanked it over his head, glaring at me. I'd never seen Liam so angry, and knowing I was the cause made me feel sick. "You weren't doing anything to fight him off. What has really been going on when he pulls you into his mind?" He demanded.

"He's been fucking with my head, I told you," I said quietly, still sitting in bed while he began pacing.

"You were almost inviting him to fuck you, from what I just saw!" I could hear his thoughts and knew he'd seen more than I realised. He'd been there long enough to hear me tell Connor I suspected he wasn't as evil as he claimed.

This meant he had seen Connor almost kiss me, and I did nothing to push him away.

Liam followed my line of thought and nodded.

"I could tell he'd pulled you in, so I went in to try and pull you out, and I found the pair of pressed up against a fucking wall!"

"It's not what you think, Liam." Yet my mind flashed involuntarily to the night before.

Liam's face dropped. His arms slackened at his sides, and I watched the fight drain out of him. He grabbed his shoes and flung the door open.

"Where are you going?"

"I can't even look at you right now." His voice shook, and I could feel the bile rise in my throat when he slammed the door behind him. I ran for the bathroom to throw up once again. Once I'd emptied the contents of my stomach, I curled up in a ball on the bathroom floor and let the tears fall, terrified that Liam would never be able to forgive me.

I wasn't even sure that I deserved his forgiveness.

Chapter Twenty-Four

I REMAINED IN OUR room for the rest of the day but took a walk when Liam still hadn't returned by the evening. I had had so few moments to myself since I transitioned, and our conversation last night had my emotions on high alert. After walking awhile, I sat on the bench that overlooked the river close to the nearest City Cat terminal and considered the water that continued to rage. There was still so much debris floating by, and I watched in silence when a large boat floated by, having broken free of its moorings. I was powerless to do anything when it slammed into the ferry terminal, and the gangway screeched loudly with the impact. Eventually, the water pushed it further, and the gangway went with it.

I just watched it all silently.

That was a strong symbol of how I was feeling inside right now.

"Interesting to see you here without Liam."

I wasn't surprised to find Eve suddenly sitting beside me, watching the boat go further downstream.

"I was wondering how long it would be before you came to find me." I returned my gaze to the river before me and waited for her to speak. Something told me she had been waiting for me to be alone.

"I wasn't sure if Liam would ever leave your side. He's quite protective of you, you know. In all our years together, I've never seen him like this over anyone."

I knew what she was doing. She needed to remind me how long she'd known him, that he was hers, long before he'd been mine.

"I don't know that I'd call what I've seen between the two you of as being together. More like a very long fuck buddy arrangement." I wouldn't allow her to believe she had any power over me.

She gave a little laugh beside me.

"No, I guess you wouldn't see it that way. He always kept himself that little bit distanced from me. I knew he was waiting for something better to come along. I should have known it would be you."

I turned and looked at her.

"Is there a reason you needed to wait for Liam to be away before we spoke?"

"We have a lot to discuss Isolde. Some of it concerns Liam, but he isn't ready to hear the hard truths just yet. He has always been quite guarded regarding myself and my family. His family, too, not that he ever wanted to admit it. He always saw himself as a member of that ridiculous Order of the Dragon first, attempting to ignore what he truly was." She wrinkled her nose in distaste.

"And what is that, exactly?"

"I'm going to tell you a little story. About how this whole mess started." While she spoke, her voice took on the lilting tones of a storyteller. We didn't look at each other when she continued, staring out at the river but lost in the past.

"This isn't in the Order's history books. Those who know the truth don't like to admit their part in how this endless war began. A few thousand years ago, around the time of the Greeks, an incredibly powerful coven of witches resided in the land now referred to as Ireland. Before there was any talk of the being known as God now and any current religions you'd be aware of.

The coven was led by the most powerful members, Sithech and his wife. Sithech was a cruel man and attempted to rule their people through fear. But his wife was fair and kind. Their people rallied behind her and tolerated Sithech only because of their love for her. And amongst her people was a man who loved her more than any other. He eventually became her lover.

Sithech knew how the rest of the coven felt about him, and he grew incredibly jealous of their loyalty to her. He flew into a rage when he learned of the relationship between his wife and her lover. They eventually overthrew him, and he was cast out of the coven. The marriage was dissolved, and he left, vowing vengeance.

But they forgot how powerful Sithech was. On the night of their marriage, whilst the coven celebrated their union, he brought a powerful curse down on them both. They awoke the night after the celebrations completely changed. Her lover became cruel, a feral creature who could no longer walk in the light and craved the blood of humans. All that remained of his former self was his passionate love for his wife, but it was an obsession now. He became the first nightwalker. And his wife... She became the first daywalker. She retained the memories of their former selves. Her love for him and her magic remained, but she was also cursed with a need for blood. But she found she was able to survive on the blood of animals.

She attempted to find ways to break the curse. But she could no longer overlook these details as he began killing those within the coven and the people in the nearby villages, turning more of them into the same violent creatures by draining them of blood. The remaining adults within the coven rallied behind her and allowed her to turn them into daywalkers as well.

They soon discovered these creatures could not be killed easily. Eventually, they learned they could only be destroyed through a silver stake to the heart, their heads being removed, or burning them. And so began a millennia-long war that has moved across the world in secret. Though their origin has become a legend and the basis of many religions."

I was brought out of my transfixed state as Eve turned to me, her eyes on my face.

"You knew the wife, didn't you?" My voice was barely more than a whisper.

After staring at me for a few moments, she eventually nodded.

"Yes. I was forced to watch the people I had loved and respected my entire life become creatures of the purest evil overnight. They ripped the villages around us apart. Those villagers had relied on us for protection from all magical and supernatural beings. Instead, we caused their demise because we could not bring ourselves to end them all. By the time we were able to, it was too late. The bloodshed had spread far and wide, and the entire cursed land was a war zone for a time. We eventually managed to limit their damage as humankind grew in number and civilisations rose."

For the first time since I had met her, her cool facade had dropped, and I could see the sadness behind her eyes.

"The children of the original coven were the first with dragon tattoos, which appeared the same night that Sithech uttered that goddamn curse. But over time, it changed to only being those within the bloodlines who were the seventh sons and daughters like they are now. They didn't band together until around eight hundred years ago. Before that, they were all random, long-lived individuals with magic in their veins, and sometimes we fought alongside them. But once the Order developed, we stopped working with them when they became so fucking high and mighty. Their histories are hidden from the vast majority, though there are one or two that would know the truth."

At some point in her story, I had twisted in my seat to gape at her, taking in everything she said. When it became apparent that I wouldn't say anything, Eve continued her story.

"As far as the Order and Liam are aware, the daywalkers who were around in the beginning have all been destroyed by the nightwalkers, but a few of us remain. We eventually were forced to turn others outside of the coven to become like us. Out of either desperation to increase our numbers or for the few who found mortals they fell in love with. But we were still vastly outnumbered by the nightwalkers. While we have eliminated many of those early nightwalkers, the curse will remain until the original players are reunited."

The point of her story was beginning to dawn on me.

"The prophecy about me, that I'll have the power to end this... It means I can kill him, doesn't it?"

She studied me once again before nodding.

"The Gemini prophecy came about around six hundred years ago. And then the Phoenix prophecy followed around fifty years later. At first, I gave them no real attention, as there had been many prophecies that all proved to be utter bullshit, spewed forth by the Order to give themselves some relevance. But then I became aware of Liam and his brother's existence, and I was intrigued. Twins where one of them was destined to be a member of the Order and males... When I came across Liam that night, I had to turn him. I couldn't risk losing the chance to set the wheels in motion in case there was any truth to it all. It didn't hurt that he was so beautiful, either. And so good between the sheets once he got past that ridiculous obsession with God," she said with a smirk.

I glared at her.

"Oh, come on, Isolde. Lighten up a little."

I felt my temper starting to flare again, and she laughed.

"That rage you have been feeling bubbling away beneath the surface? That is key to all of this. You carry the powers of both bloodlines within you now," she said.

I'm pretty sure time stood still while I tried to comprehend what she'd just revealed.

"I... what?!"

"It's why you see the memories from all of them. You needed to be fed on by all three of them to activate the powers fully during your transition."

I stared at her in shock.

Chapter Twenty-Five

"S o, I'm what? Some sort of fucked hybrid?!"

She shrugged like she hadn't just dropped a massive revelation in my lap.

I took a deep breath, pushing the shock aside as best I could.

"How did you manage to keep all of this from Liam when he has your blood memories?"

"I can choose which memories are seen by those I turn," she said.

I was reminded of my most recent exchange with Connor.

"I didn't know that was possible," I said, my concern growing.

"Only a few of us have that power," she said with a shrug.

How did Connor have that power?

"Do I have that power?"

"Perhaps. You have already proven your power, even before you were turned. I've heard about your fire abilities whilst you've been out patrolling this last week. The original coven had similar powers, as well as the ability to move objects with their minds, amongst many others." She looked at the river again and nodded towards a tree moving towards where we were sitting.

"Use your telekinesis on that. Liam mentioned that you had previously been trying to work on it but could only really get things to move slightly. Is that correct?"

I looked at her, wondering what else she and Liam had spoken about. No one seemed to have told her I needed his touch to control my abilities. After a brief hesitation, I nodded, and she waved towards the river.

"Try using it now to stop that tree from continuing down the river."

I hesitated for a few moments before focusing on the tree. In the few months before my transition, the most I'd been able to do was get a vase to shake a little and the occasional accidental door slam, though I had spent many hours trying. It had only been with Liam's assistance that I'd been able to move anything properly.

I took a deep breath and concentrated on the tree, staring at it while it passed us by, expecting it to continue. Instead, it stopped abruptly, the water flowing around it while it floated in place.

At first, it didn't move at all, but gradually, my mind began to fatigue, and it began to move inch by inch. I tried to maintain my concentration, but eventually, I lost focus, and the tree continued on its way once more while I gasped for air, having expended all my energy. I felt my need for blood spike once more, and the burning in my throat returned with force. I felt my eyes water while the hunger consumed me, and Eve raised her wrist to my mouth.

"Feed."

I didn't hesitate and bit into her wrist, beginning to drink hungrily. I realised how intimate our current position was when the hunger started to wane. She had her other arm around me while I sat so close that I might as well be sitting in her lap. Her hand was tangled in my hair, with her lips pressed to my temple. Anyone walking by would have seen two lovers in an embrace.

I pushed her hand away, and she let her arm fall to her lap, the amusement at my reaction evident in her eyes. There was something about this woman's power over those around her, like moths drawn to a flame.

I didn't like it.

"What's going on?"

I ripped my gaze from Eve's to find Liam standing behind her. I knew her blood was still on my lips when he took in how we were both sitting wrapped together. For her part, Eve merely turned to look up at him, her grip holding me to her. My insides churned at being found in yet another compromising position.

"Just getting to know Isolde. And sharing some information." She removed her hand from my hair, but not before she turned to brush her lips against my temple once again, giving the air of comforting a lover. She shifted slightly before standing gracefully, and Liam's gaze fell to her wrist, which had already begun to heal, before returning to look her in the eye.

"And just how did you share this information, Eve?" His words were low and lethal, but Eve merely smiled at him before walking towards him and stroking his arm. She wielded her sexuality like a weapon, and I noted a slight shudder pass through his body that Liam could not hide. She turned to look back at me once more, her hand moving up his neck and pulling his head down to hers so that she could bring their lips together in a demanding kiss that he didn't immediately push away from. Her eyes remained open and held my gaze the entire time while she kissed him hungrily, pressing her body into his before Liam finally had the presence of mind to push her away and step back, his eyes full of warning. She smiled at us both.

"Leave Eve. Now." Liam's voice shook, and she laughed, low and intimate.

"I'll be seeing you both soon. Real soon." She turned and finally walked away, and I felt the weight of her presence begin to lift. I remember her words from a few days ago, telling me she was more powerful than I was. I knew without any doubt that I couldn't trust her.

Liam stalked over to stand before me before dropping to his knees and pulling me roughly to him, crushing my mouth with his own. Like he needed to remove the memory of Eve and that kiss from our minds. I returned the intensity, clinging to him like he was a life raft amongst the insanity I had just been exposed to, but I felt a memory beginning to drag me away, and he held me up when I collapsed forward into him.

I woke to the smell of blood and immediately jumped to my feet. I surveyed the room I was in but saw nothing out of place. I moved into the next room of our shelter, the ample gathering space where, only the night before, Adhamh and

I had exchanged our vows before our children, the rest of the coven, and the villagers from nearby. A few bodies still lay around the room where our guests had fallen asleep, having dropped in exhaustion after hours of celebration. We had invited those from the surrounding settlements that we continued to protect from the darkness with our magic.

I tripped over the body of one of those villagers now, their form only just visible in the darkness that blanketed the space. I bent to shake them awake, but they didn't move, and when I touched their arm, there was no warmth to their skin. I swallowed hard while I conjured a small ball of fire in my hand and brought it closer to the still form on the ground. In the light of the flame, I could see that the woman on the floor was dead, her throat having been torn completely open in a way I had never seen before. Her head had been almost completely ripped from her body, and I struggled to keep down the bile that rose from my stomach. There was a strange burning in my throat, but I ignored it as best as possible while I willed the flame to grow larger, allowing me to see more of the gathering space. I turned slowly in place, surveying the room and the rest of the bodies that lay around the room. Every single person had the same sickening wounds.

Frantically, I raced to each body to see if any remained alive, but they were all dead. How had I slept through their screams? Where were my children? And where was Adhamh?

I ran outside and saw that dawn would soon break on the horizon. Other members of the coven emerged, and we all gathered, the horror beginning to dawn on us as we followed the trail of bodies. It seemed as though only those in the main shelter and outside had been attacked. Those within the smaller shelters appeared to have remained unscathed.

"I have never seen anything like this. What could have done this to them?" Siobhan asked tearfully.

I hugged her close, my eyes searching the faces of those around me, and I sagged with relief as I saw my twin daughters, Eireann and Isla, step out of Siobhan's shelter. My son, Daemon, had chosen to leave with his father months ago, and I silently prayed to the mother that he was safe. Adhamh's twin sons, Aden and Chey, stood amongst the young men who had gathered together, taking protective stances around the younger children, ready to protect them against whatever evil had managed to penetrate the protective wards around our homes.

"I don't know. I don't know," I whispered. I couldn't think straight, the burning in my throat becoming unbearable. Over Siobhan's shoulder, my eyes drifted to a rabbit peeking out of the nearby thicket of trees. Moving at a speed I didn't know I possessed, I instantly fell upon it, sinking my teeth into it while it kicked and screamed fruitlessly. I drained it of blood until it stopped shrieking and twitching. Coming back to myself, I dropped it in horror and stared down at my shaking hands before looking up into the eyes of the others while they surveyed my actions, their faces pale.

"What evil is this?" Aoife whispered, and I began to shake uncontrollably when they all gathered together, some raising their hands, ready to protect themselves from whatever I had become.

Maeve saw him first, calling everyone's attention to the path from our home to the village closest to us. As one, we turned to see Adhamh, and I cried out his name, rising to my feet, tears streaming down my face.

"What has happened?" I rushed towards him and threw my arms around his neck. He wrapped his arms around me and held me close, breathing in my scent, and I felt his body relax into mine.

"There now, love. I have returned." I continued clinging to him while the others watched us closely. Many seemed to grow even more uneasy while they just stared at Adhamh.

I stepped back and took in Adhamh's appearance properly for the first time since he had entered the clearing.

He was coated in blood, and I covered my mouth to stop the scream from escaping when I took in the changed eye colour, a feral gleam to them when he reached for me again. I became aware of the evil presence that drifted off of him. I don't know how I had managed to miss that in my relief at seeing his return, but now it was so strong that I could do nothing but slowly walk backwards from him as he continued holding his arms out to me.

"Aoibh, what is it, my love?" There was something about his voice. Almost like a predator attempting to lure its prey with a false sense of safety.

When he advanced, I used my powers to throw up a shield between us and called my coven to my side. Thankfully, between myself and Adhamh, they saw me as the lesser of two evils and moved to stand behind me, throwing up their shields.

That Adhamh was unable to break through our shields was another shock. Our powers had always been evenly matched, yet he seemed unable to produce even the smallest amount of magic to push back against us.

"What are you?" My words were a whisper in the wind, and I was thrown by the laughter that answered me.

Sithech stepped out of the woods behind Adhamh. We had not seen him for weeks, not since the council had voted him out, and he had left, spitting threats while he passed.

"You should have known better than to believe that I wouldn't find some way to punish you for the humiliation you brought upon me, Aoibh." He gestured towards where Adhamh stood, attempting to find some way around the shields we had cast around ourselves and the children. Adhamh's sons had begun to cry silently from where they stood at my side.

"What have you done, Sithech?" Maeve yelled, and Sithech laughed again.

"I have cursed them both. I replaced Adhamh's magic with a lust for the blood of man. He will know no rest for all eternity. Will never again feel the sun upon his face. But I made sure he still knew his love for you, Aoibh. Love that will consume him, along with his need for blood." He gestured towards where Adhamh watched me hungrily.

"And what of Aoibh?" Siobhan asked, her voice trembling.

"She will be forced to walk the earth for as long as Adhamh does, knowing this is all her fault." He pointed at me, the smile on his face showing the madness within. "Animals may sate your hunger for blood, as you have already noticed, unlike his. But you exist to balance his evil. There always needs to be a balance, as we all know."

Magic did require a balance amongst all aspects of nature, and clearly, the way to balance the pure evil he had inflicted on Adhamh was by placing a curse upon me to keep him from becoming a scourge upon the earth. Sithech shifted his focus onto Adhamh now.

"You took what was mine. This is the consequence of your actions, brother."

Adhamh ignored his words, continuing to watch me and only me.

"Better run along now. The sun is almost up, and you don't want to see what happens if you are caught out in the daylight." His words were like a command, and Adhamh slowly moved back into the woods, disappearing into the darkness that was beginning to make way for the dawn.

"Goodbye, Aoibh. It is now on you to ensure he doesn't destroy everything we built together." He threw his shield up when Maeve flung a ball of flame at him, and he disappeared into the darkness, leaving us all to deal with the fallout of one man's jealousy.

I could only pray to the mother that this would not be the end of Adhamh and me, that I could find some way out of this curse to save the man I loved.

I shook free of the memory and found myself wrapped in Liam's arms. He sat with me in his lap, stroking my hair while waiting for me to return. I hated how vulnerable these memory flashes were making me, and I was just grateful that they hadn't occurred when I was in mortal danger. I prayed that it would continue.

Liam must have noticed the change in me, reaching down to lift my chin so that I could look him in the eye.

"What did you see?"

I took a deep breath, trying to understand what I had just seen.

"Eve told me to feed off her when my bloodlust set in. Although I suspect now, she set everything up for you to see or force me to see that memory...." My voice trailed off when Liam's expression hardened. He shifted me off his lap to sit beside him.

"What did you see?" His tone was strained as he repeated the question, and I reached up to touch his face. He pulled away from my touch, and I let my hand fall to my side.

I knew what I was about to say would blow everything he'd ever believed apart.

And that Eve hadn't been as honest with me as she'd claimed. I wondered if she'd meant for me to see that memory.

"Did you know Eve was the original daywalker, Liam?" He stared at me, his eyes wide.

"What? No, she isn't... She can't be... I'd know..." His words were pleading, and he shook his head. "I would know, Isolde."

There was no time to ease him into all that I now knew, and I repeated the story that Eve had told me earlier, my heart breaking as yet more of the truths that had been held from him were laid bare. I wondered how much more he could take, but I ploughed on, needing to share what I now knew and had seen in the memory. When I told him about my hybrid vampire status, Liam's face turned pale, and it was a long time before he responded. I watched while he processed everything, taking it all in.

"So, her finding me that night was no coincidence? She knew of the Gemini Prophecy?" I nodded slowly, and he let out a shaky breath. After a moment, he helped me get to my feet, standing beside me while he ran both hands through his hair before leaning his forearms on the walkway railing and staring across the river. The vein in his neck pounded while he gritted his teeth.

"Did she explain what our role in all of this is meant to be? Aside from your powers? Connor and I must play a part in this too, and Aurora... We have to if it was us that activated your powers." He glanced at me when I moved to stand beside him, mirroring his stance. I shook my head, and he exhaled, turning away again.

"We didn't get that far in the conversation. But, from her words as she left, I guess we'll find out soon enough."

"I fucking hate this. I hate all of this. I've spent over five hundred years living with all this knowledge that now turns out to be a lie. I don't even know who the fuck I am." He stared at his hands, the anger and frustration coming off him in waves. If it had been anyone else, I would have wanted to step away, fearing what he might do. But I reached up and placed my hand on his cheek, relieved when he leaned into my touch instead of pulling away, allowing me to give him the small comfort I could.

"I know who you are, Liam. And there is nothing that I turn away from. We face all of this shit together, remember?"

He looked at me again, studying my face for the longest time like he was trying to memorise every feature.

His mind was such a jumble of thoughts that I couldn't catch any of them.

"I don't know if we are together in this anymore, Isolde. I can't just ignore what has been happening with you and Connor and that you've lied to me. With everything we've learned these past few weeks, you had to know that I needed your honesty. And yet you chose to keep the fact that my brother has been seducing you in your dreams... That you allowed him to kiss and touch you in ways that..." He looked down at his hands that were clenched into fists before him. "We've never discussed monogamy, but I assumed it was implied... And for it to be with my twin brother, who I have been at war with for over five hundred years... I don't think I can get past this." I could feel my heart breaking at his words, and the panic inside me started rising when he stepped away from me.

"Please, Liam. You have to understand that when he pulls me into his mind, I lose all control of who I am. I think he can tap into some part of me that I'm unaware exists and use it against me." I was begging now. I moved towards him to touch his face once again, but he stepped away from my hand, and I let it drop to my side.

"You're it for me, Liam." I could feel tears starting to build behind my eyes.

"I need time, Isolde. These past few weeks have been a lot, and now, knowing everything that has been going on... I don't think I can trust anything you do right now. There is obviously so much more happening here than I ever imagined," Liam said, and I could hear his thoughts bouncing from one thing to another. I had wondered how much more he could handle and knew he'd reached his breaking point.

"I love you, Liam. You know that... I know you know that." I wanted to grab him and never let go, terrified of what I knew would happen.

"I don't think that's enough right now." He took one final step back when I reached towards him again. "I just... I'll see you later, Isolde."

My heart shattered when he turned and walked away again.

Chapter Twenty-Six

I STAYED THERE FOR hours, praying Liam would eventually return. But I knew in my heart that when he'd said he needed time, he didn't mean a few hours. He meant days, weeks, years... Possibly an eternity.

I struggled to keep myself together and knew that staying here wouldn't make it any better. So I got to my feet and began walking when the sun rose.

I had no idea how long I had been walking for or even where I was going. My mind was a jumbled mess of everything that had happened over the past few weeks. I wish I understood how Connor drew me to him and why I let him do things I would usually never do. This wasn't who I was. I didn't cheat. Liam had my entire heart.

When I finally stopped walking, I wasn't even slightly surprised to find myself standing in front of that abandoned house where Connor and Aurora had held me captive weeks ago and attempted to turn me. Part of me knew why I was there and who would be standing inside waiting for me. And yet, I couldn't stop myself from stepping through the door.

Connor and I studied each other closely when I entered the room and found him sitting exactly where I expected.

In that damn chair.

The fear I had once felt had long been replaced by something else. He didn't say anything at first. He just watched me while I looked at him. It was scary how much he looked like his brother. I fought to control the pain in my heart at the thought of Liam.

"I'm more like my twin than he'd like to admit." I felt my eyebrows rise at his words, and he smirked. "No, I didn't read your thoughts. I could just tell what you were thinking. Seeing into your thoughts outside of our shared dreams is a luxury only my brother has."

"Why do you hate him so much? I know that there is something inside of you that still has access to human emotion," I said, and he crossed his arms when he sat back in the chair again, studying me closely for a few moments.

"So, you've worked me out, have you, Isolde? Is that why you're here? To convince me that I made the wrong choice?" He cocked his head to the side, and I felt my stomach plummet at the expression on his face. Choice. That word confirmed my suspicions about myself for the last few weeks, and I struggled to control my emotions.

"So I'm right? You are like me, a fucked up hybrid of the two bloodlines." He raised a finger to his lips.

"Ssshhh. Correction. I was once like you. But I made my choice, just like you eventually will. It will be interesting which way you decide to go... Take the path of duty and honour... or the path that leads to eternal pleasure." He let the word roll off his tongue in a way that made it clear what sort of pleasure he was alluding to, but I wouldn't allow him to distract me.

"No, you are still like me. I can feel it. You think you've switched that side of you off, but it's still there, just beneath the surface. You try to make out that you're this evil badass... But really... You spend each day fighting a war within yourself." I felt this with absolute certainty.

Connor's eyes flashed before he smirked at me once more. He used his vampire speed to stand before me in a fraction of a second and lifted a strand of my hair, rolling it between his fingers while he gazed at it. I held myself perfectly still, and he eventually looped my hair back behind my ear, his fingers lingering when they brushed my throat.

"You're so convinced that you know me. But I think you have me confused with my gallant younger brother. He was always the moral centre... I was the one who had fun." He took my hand and turned it over, tracing his finger over the different lines. He looked back at me from under his long lashes. "Don't you just want to have fun, Isolde?" He smiled seductively, and I fought to ignore the stirrings of attraction within myself.

He's not Liam, I mentally chastised myself.

Connor laughed. "Oh, Isolde, I have so much fun with you. I can't wait to see how long it takes before you finally give in to me."

"I hate to disappoint you, Connor, but I have no intention of ever being involved with you. I've never been the type to go for the bad boy." I removed my hand from his, growing annoyed with his constant games and innuendo, knowing it was all just a smoke screen. He moved closer to my side and kissed my cheek.

"You say that now. But you forget, Isolde, I know what's happening within you. I remember all too well how the conflict currently warring inside your pretty little head feels." He brought his lips close to my ear, and the feeling of his breath on my neck sent a shiver down my spine that I couldn't suppress.

"And in your heart." He placed his hand on my chest, where I knew he could feel my heart thundering away. I wished his touch repelled me, but the part I had been fighting to suppress was drawn to him and everything he represented.

"Eventually, you'll want to know what living as I do feels like. Without the weight of the world on your shoulders. You have no idea." He started to kiss my neck, and I had to fight to pull myself away. Eventually, I got a hold of myself and stepped out of his reach.

"I know this is all an act, Connor, and I don't buy it for a second. You forget that I know that you also retain the ability to walk in the daylight." I pointed to the window that he currently stood in front of. "You stand in the sun's rays and do not so much as flinch. So you can keep pretending that Liam is the only one still possessing his morality. Just know that I know the truth." I turned and walked away, praying that I was right... And a small part of me wondered what would have happened if I had just given in.

I walked a little further before reaching a park near my parent's house. My sisters and I had played here countless times as children, and I sat down on one of the benches overlooking the playground, lost in thought.

My phone rang in my pocket, and I pulled it out, seeing Mum's name on the screen. I had forgotten I even had it on me and considered ignoring it. But it was the first time she had called me since I'd left them all at Briseis and Dean's house, and something told me this wasn't just a catch-up call.

"Hello?"

"Oh, thank god you answered." Mum's words came out in a jumble. I could hear the emotion in her voice and felt my grip on the phone tighten.

"What's happened?"

"Aurora attempted to attack the house last night. When she didn't get in, she went to one of her friends' places and got an invite." I felt my blood run cold when she started crying.

"Who?" I whispered, lifting my eyes to look up at the sky.

"It was John's place. Jacob was staying there." I knew what she was going to say next.

"She killed Jacob, didn't she?"

"Yes." She said with a loud sob and completely broke down. Dad's voice replaced hers a moment later.

"She killed John and his family as well." His voice was rough, and I tried not to imagine how they were all standing together right now.

"What is Ainslie saying is happening with the Order?"

"She said they will handle it, whatever the fuck that means." Dad never swore, and I wished, for the thousandth time, that I could spare them all from this grief. The same grief that was tearing me apart inside.

"I'll find out what's going on. I'm so sorry, Dad." I managed to say before I hung up and began to cry in earnest.

I shouldn't have been surprised that this exchange and memories of my twin caused the now-familiar sensation of being pulled into a memory.

I kissed Jacob goodbye, more out of habit than anything else. I'd barely been holding it together since my argument with Isolde earlier this morning. I was grateful that Jacob had plans without me so that I could cry without anyone else around.

Ever since Will had died, it was like I was living inside a black pit of despair. And because no one knew of the true nature of our relationship, I couldn't even mourn him openly as Isolde had. Not that she seemed to have done much in the way of mourning. She was already rolling around between the sheets with someone else only months after his death. Sure, Liam was fucking hot, but how do you go from being madly in love with one guy who was murdered in front of you to suddenly jumping into bed with another? And I seriously doubted that this was a new thing. He seemed to know her pretty damn well for someone she's just started talking about. And who the hell were all the other people who had been trekking through the house the past few weeks?

I had never heard her mention any of these people before. Something didn't add up.

I went into my cupboard and pulled out the jumper of Will's that I had smuggled out of one of the boxes when Isolde wasn't looking and breathed in the lingering scent of him once again. When would the pain of his death ease?

Tears began running down my face, and I curled into a ball on the floor, sobbing hard. I gripped his jumper to my chest, despairing that this was all I had left of him. How could someone so full of life just be gone? Without having the chance to really live?

Eventually, my sobs eased, and I finally sat up. The smell of burning fabric reached my nose, and I looked down to see a puff of smoke coming from the material still gripped in my fist. I cautiously opened my hand and gasped at the sight of the burnt fabric. How the fuck had that happened? I threw the jumper away from me and stared at it in horror.

Back in my own thoughts, I stared at my right hand, confused at what I had just seen. How had she managed to do that? Aurora didn't have any powers...

I continued walking for the rest of the day, dealing with the latest round of grief that Jacob's death had unleashed and the guilt of being unable to prevent it. I wasn't ready to return to Eve's house and face being there without Liam, and I was still puzzling over the memory from Aurora.

As dusk began to fall, I stopped in front of a park I had been driving past my whole life. It was the same park where Liam had told me the truth about who I was only a few short months ago, although it felt like a lifetime now.

I walked over to the picnic table where we had sat that night, lying on top of the table and staring at the sky when the stars began to appear.

How had everything become so complicated? Life had been simple once. Like many other women in love, I'd been floating through life without any real problems. And then the world exploded, reality hit, and everything became so much worse. Now, I was living out some internal battle within my mind, one half of me wanting to give in to the darkness, to stop feeling everything so deeply. The other half of me was screaming to do the right thing, return to the daywalkers, join forces with the Order, and wage war against an evil army.

"It doesn't have to be this hard, you know?" A voice came out of the darkness, and I jumped up so quickly that I would have been dizzy if I had been human.

It appeared that Connor was able to sneak up on me. I remembered now that he had somehow hidden an entire room full of nightwalkers from me a few weeks ago, but something told me this was different when he stepped out of the shadows. Despite the darkness, I could see him clear as day, the benefits of superhuman vision.

"What doesn't have to be so hard?" I clenched my jaw and willed my body to behave when Connor came to stand beside me. I hated how my body reacted whenever Connor came near me, like something within me hungered for his touch.

He leaned back against the table, crossing his arms and turning to look at me. I focused on my breathing, refusing to give in, and I could tell he was enjoying the effect he was having on me.

Bastard.

"Making the decision. It would be so much easier if you just gave in. That's what I did. And believe me, life, or un-life if you will, has been much simpler. There has been none of the soul-searching nonsense you have been feeling, just simply living for the pleasures and ignoring the crap."

I groaned, throwing my head up to stare up at the stars.

"Stop feeding me the bullshit line that you don't care about anything. You keep forgetting that I've seen your memories. I know full well that this is all an act. You haven't made any damn choice. You just put up the façade of being evil so that you don't have to deal with all the crap you struggle with daily." I went to walk away from him, but he reached out and caught my hand, turning me to face him.

"Alright then. So what emotion am I feeling right now, oh wise one?" There was a dangerous glint in his eye. Like he was daring me to tell him the truth about who he was.

"You're scared."

"I think your radar is a little broken." He scoffed.

"No, it's not. You're scared. You don't know how to deal with what I force you to feel. You've never met another hybrid like you, and now that I've come along, it's forced you to deal with all the crap you've been suppressing for centuries. And it scares the hell out of you." His jaw clenched, and his eyes flashed. His hands balled into fists, the one holding mine squeezing my fingers painfully.

"I'm not the one you want to strike out at, Connor. You're angry at everyone and everything. Life would be easier for you if you were filled with the mindless hunger of a nightwalker, but you have emotions. You do feel, possibly even deeper than a human. It's our curse." I stepped closer to him, his hand still gripping mine, forcing him to look into my eyes. I was tired of him always being the one to talk, to tell me how I was feeling and give in to the hunger, to run away from the pain that the conflict inside caused.

He searched my eyes for a moment, the anger still boiling beneath the surface, though I could feel something else within him stirring. His other hand reached up and worked its way through the hair at the back of my head, and before I knew what was happening, he was kissing me.

My initial response was to pull away, but that thought flew out of my mind when I kissed him back with the same hunger and intensity that drove him. Maybe it was his emotions feeding my own, but I knew that a part of me had wanted to do this since I had woken up to this nightmare. Without knowing how I got there, I was lying back on the table with Connor on top of me, kissing my neck, sending chills down my spine.

"You want to understand why I made my decisions, Isolde? Let me show you." He whispered in my ear before pulling back and looking down at me.

I blinked, stunned by his sudden absence on top of me. It took me a moment to realise what he was offering when he placed his wrist at my mouth.

"Bite."
So I did.

Chapter Twenty-Seven

I STARED AT THE *beautiful woman before me, sitting across the table in the tavern I frequented nightly to escape the monotonous life of learning to run the family estate I had little care for. I often wished I had been born second, without any expectations of me, like Liam. I had no desire to marry and force some poor woman to start producing an army children, which had been the expectation placed upon my parents.*

"I've been watching you, little Lord." She smiled seductively, her black hair coiled high upon her head. A woman like this did not belong in a tavern such as this one. Her finery caused her to stand out amongst the men and women packed inside, avoiding the cold winter night. But then, most women of such apparent wealth did not, in my experience, tend to undress you with their eyes in private, let alone amongst a boisterous crowd of rough men and women.

"Have you now? And why is that?" I reached across the table and took her hand, bringing it to my lips to press a kiss to the back of it slowly. I was well-versed in the ways of the

female sex and had danced this dance a few times. But this woman was vastly different from those I had taken upstairs in the past. I needed to play this little courtship differently. She needed to be wooed and seduced.

"You intrigue me. I wish to get to know you better." Her eyes told me exactly how she wanted me to know her better.

"Should we go somewhere quieter then? Do you have a room upstairs?"

A woman like this surely wasn't travelling alone, so I was surprised when she nodded coyly. Without caring about the looks we received from those around us, she took me by the hand and guided me towards the stairs that led up to the rooms above. Something inside me told me that a woman who cared so little about what society thought of her was dangerous, but I was too intrigued to turn away now.

She led me to her room above the noisy tavern. It was one of the nicer ones. I'd rarely been in this room. The other rooms were better suited for the brief interludes I required them for, and this one was usually occupied by the lesser nobles who had stopped for the night whilst on their travels – the mystery of who this woman was deepened. But I didn't have a chance to think on this more as she turned and pressed me back against the door once it closed behind me. Her lips met mine hungrily, and I kissed her back. I was unaccustomed to women being so forthright, but I was more than happy to allow her to control this situation.

She deftly removed my shirt, and I turned her roughly to begin unlacing the back of her dress. The outfits that noble women wore were so damn hard to remove, and it took far longer than I would have preferred. Eventually, we were both naked and lying on the bed.

"You are so beautiful," she said while she straddled my hips and hungrily kissed my face and neck, rubbing against me. It was more than evident that this woman was no maiden, and I knew I was at risk of losing my heart without even knowing her name. I was already painfully hard, and I groaned when she eased down upon my shaft and began riding me slowly, running her hands over her ample breasts. She moaned as she rolled her hips, holding my gaze the entire time. It was almost a religious experience, and I gripped her hips, urging her to move faster while I stared up at her. She leaned forward to press her chest to mine and kissed me, slower than before, before running her lips down my throat.

"Who are you?" I whispered breathlessly, feeling my release build as she moved her hips faster, her lips pressed to my neck. She ground herself down, moving her hips in a slow, circular motion, and I felt my eyes roll back in my head. I had never experienced anything like this before, and I knew I was ruined for all other women.

"You'll find out soon enough," she whispered back, and I was too far gone to be concerned about what she meant. Pleasure shot through me just as a sharp pain began radiating up my neck, starting beneath her lips. I was dimly aware that she had bitten me, and her bite somehow drew the euphoria out while she drank from my neck. My brain screamed that this was wrong, but I was powerless to do anything, with the pleasure continuing to rock through me while she sought her own release, prolonging my own never-ending orgasm. She moaned against my neck while she continued to draw the blood from my throat, her orgasm rolling through her and causing her to shake. I began to feel lightheaded, but still, something stopped me from fighting

her off, and my eyes gradually closed when she slowed her movements, her lips remaining at my throat.

Distantly, I was aware of the door opening and someone entering the room, and she finally sat up. I couldn't find the energy to open my eyes but vaguely heard a man's voice.

"Aoibh, my love? Did you summon me? But what is this?" I felt her move off me, my mind slipping further into the darkness as she spoke.

"I have a gift for you, Adhamh. A peace offering. Doesn't he remind you of Aden and Chey? He has a twin, too." There was silence now, and I tried to fight off the fall into the whirling black, but another, more intense pain began at my throat, and the darkness claimed me.

I blinked, and the memory faded. I returned to myself with Connor's wrist still held to my lips. He had sat me up while I was in the memory and now held me against his chest while I sat sideways in his lap.

"Eve? It was Eve and Adam who turned you?" I searched Connor's face for answers, unable to believe what I had just seen. To say that I was shocked by Eve's involvement was an understatement. I'd always assumed Adam was his sire, but knowing that the daywalker involved was Eve was more than I could have ever imagined.

Could a memory from his blood be faked?

"There is far more for you to see, little one. Keep going." He urged me to continue feeding from his wrist, and I bit down again, immediately slipping into another memory.

Chapter Twenty-Eight

I GENUINELY BELIEVE THAT *a year ago, I awoke in hell. I was surrounded by the most evil creatures imaginable. Although I appeared to be the same as them, I still clung to the vestiges of humanity that remained inside me. For the last twelve months, I had been expected to follow along with the rest of the coven and was drawn to the man who controlled them all. They were all sadistic killers, and I have watched while many of them fed so brutally that they ripped the heads of their victims off with their ferocity. I hadn't been able to bring myself to kill anyone yet and hid this fact from the others by going into their feeble minds and changing what they thought they had seen. It was a talent I had discovered by accident, but I had used it to my advantage for months.*

"Your brother will have his powers within the Order activated soon. Is it not your twenty-fifth birthday tomorrow?" Adhamh asked, watching, bored, while one of the others fed hungrily off the young prostitute he had brought back to the estate Adhamh had claimed. The bodies of the previous

owners were rotting away in the unused kitchen, their heads having been torn from their shoulders and now lying in the dry-store cupboard. I never went in there, having only made that mistake once.

"I have long stopped tracking the days," I replied, my tone bored while I lied through my teeth. I knew what day it was and what that meant for my brother. I had learned much since entering this endless nightmare, including that my brother was fated to become my mortal enemy. I didn't understand why I seemed so different from the other night-walkers I was surrounded by, but I knew my sheltered younger brother was not ready to face the creatures that stalked the darkness. He had always been so devout in his belief in God, a being that I had long ago come to believe was not as accurate as the priests claimed, and I now knew to be a complete fairytale.

"We will pay him a visit tomorrow night, you and I." I felt my heart stop briefly, something else I had managed to keep hidden from those around me. I was the only one who continued to have a heartbeat and draw breath, but I also used my abilities to hide this from them all.

"Why? Surely the Order will have already drawn him into their circle?"

"I have been watching, and they are still following their usual pattern and waiting for him to be ready before informing him of his destiny. It truly is laughable." I knew there was no arguing and agreed to accompany Adhamh to my former home the following night, wondering how to save my brother from joining me in this living hell.

I kept my arms locked around Liam's upper body, playing my part well while I fought the internal war raging within me as we watched Adhamh tear our mother's throat out. Liam was no match for my strength while I held him tight, though I was impressed at the effort he was putting in nonetheless.

Perhaps having my brother at my side through this nightmare wouldn't be so bad. With any luck, he will be like me, and together, we could gain control of the coven and bring the madness to an end.

I allowed the daydream to help me escape the reality of my situation while Adhamh turned his attention from our mother to my brother, who had now gone rigid in my arms, the scent of his fear filling the air.

Adhamh stepped forward, his gaze falling upon my brother, who began to whimper in my arms. The sound of glass shattering distracted us both, and I looked over to see Callum pointing a crossbow at me through the window. I swore and let go of Liam, who dropped to the ground and landed in the pool of our mother's blood. Adhamh was already fleeing the room, and I wondered briefly if this many people would be what it took to kill him finally. The villagers behind Callum held torches, and I wasn't interested in seeing what would happen if he managed to use better aim with the next bolt. His eyes were set on me while I watched him reload. I looked down at Liam again before hastily following Adhamh out the door.

Adhamh was already long gone, and I knew he would leave me to make my own way back. I aimed for the trees behind the manor but heard a noise behind me. I turned towards it, seeing Liam racing away from the servant's entrance, covered in blood. I ran after him, although I was unsure of what I would do once I found him. He couldn't know what I had become, or the Order would come after me, and I had managed to avoid them so far. But perhaps I could get him to see what I truly was, and he could help me find a way out of this mess.

I followed Liam, remaining silent, waiting to see where he was going. He stumbled upon the ruined church on the outer edge of our estate, one neither of us had known about in our youth, but I'd discovered in my wanderings when I was older. When he didn't appear after some time, I eased my way inside and came upon a scene I had not expected. There was the woman who had started me on this path to madness, feeding from my brother, who lay upon the altar.

"You!" I yelled, expecting her to look up, but she simply raised a hand toward me, and I flew back against the wall, unable to move while some invisible force kept me there. I struggled to free myself but was no match for whatever magic she possessed. I heard my brother's heart slow and eventually cease to beat. She finally looked up, wiping the blood from her mouth, and released the magic that had kept me pinned against the wall. I moved quickly and appeared at her side, grabbing her roughly by the hair and pulling her away from Liam's lifeless body.

"Who the fuck are you?"

She looked up at me with such a condescending smile that I considered punching her, but I knew that I was no match for her.

"Why are you doing this to my family?"

"You have much to learn, dear boy. The wheels are now in motion, and it is time you understood your part." She placed a hand on my cheek, and I was stunned by the sadness I saw behind her eyes.

"What do you mean, my part? You're the one who is doing all of this."

"I had to. This has all gone on for far too long. And it needs to end. This is how it has to be. It is all that I can do." And she began to explain some prophecy about twins and ending the nightwalkers once and for all.

"Why are you telling me this? I'm a nightwalker?! Why would I be involved in ending them."

"You know that isn't true, Connor. You are different to them. Have you not worked this out?" She looked at me with pity in her eyes, and I growled.

"Speak plainly, devil woman." I shook her roughly, tired of all these games.

"You are a hybrid. The first of your kind. Created to activate the spell."

"Spell? I thought you said it was a prophecy."

She laughed.

"That's what everyone needs to believe. But it is a spell. Just like this whole mess started because of a spell. And once the second set of twins come along, and the most powerful of you all is turned, becoming a hybrid like you, the spell will be cast. She will finally end this miserable existence with fire in her heart." Her words meant nothing to me, but she continued to speak regardless of the confusion on my face.

"There needed to be balance, darkness and light. There always needs to be a balance."

It was like coming into the story halfway through without anyone explaining what had occurred in the beginning. And none of it made sense.

"What the fuck are you talking about?!"

"You were never meant to exist!"

I stared at her while she threw her hands up in the air.

"Start from the beginning, woman. You are making absolutely no sense. Clearly, I exist. I'm standing right here."

She took a deep breath and glared at me for a moment. I could almost see the wheels in her brain turning.

"We have been attempting to end the curse of the nightwalkers for a millennium. But we have been unable to stop their spread until now. A spell was cast to bring the pair of you into existence, to ensure that Liam would have the power of a seventh son of a seventh son. But he also needed a twin who possessed the dark side to his light. Who shared a womb with him. To share his power and play his own part in the spell." She gestured towards me, and I fought against the emotions these words stirred.

I had always known that Liam was a better man than me, but to have someone refer to me as his darker side was like a knife to the gut.

"This was the only way to have both men capable of wielding the powers of the original coven. Specifically, from Adhamh's bloodline," she said.

My mind was reeling from all this information, most of which still made no sense to me.

"What about this other set of twins you were rambling about? Where are they?"

"They will not be born for many years yet. It took us centuries to have everything exactly right to create you and Liam."

"Centuries? Surely you can't be serious?"

"Such powerful magic always has a price. In this instance, that price is time. But when the female twins are born, the one with the full powers of the Order will be the one to bring it all to an end. She will be more powerful than any of us combined, with the bloodlines of the strongest members of the original coven running through her veins. She will become a hybrid, like you."

"What of Liam and the other female twin? Are they to be hybrids as well?" I prayed she would say yes, that Liam would somehow be changed like I was, and I wouldn't be alone with this knowledge for centuries.

"Liam will awaken as a daywalker in seven days. I have just started his transition now. The other female will become a nightwalker, so we have a twin on either side."

"Let me guess - so that they balance each other out?" I was starting to hate the word balance.

"You're catching on quick, Connor." She patted my cheek, and I felt my eyes flash.

"Why can't I just kill the nightwalkers, then? Or you, for that matter?" I didn't understand why this all needed to be done in such an elaborate and fucked up way.

"You don't have the power to kill Adhamh on your own. No single nightwalker, daywalker or Order member does. This was the only way I could create beings with the power to do so. You are simply the first step. But you must remain at Adhamh's side to ensure all the pieces are right once the time comes."

"I don't understand why I needed to be the hybrid. Surely it should be Liam if he's got the powers of the Order." There seemed to be so many loopholes in her logic.

"You and Liam are two halves of the same whole. Surely you have worked out that you have powers that no other nightwalker has? The ability to control minds and enter dreams? Liam has similar powers. Yours were activated by the spell when you became a hybrid, and Liam's were activated by his turning twenty-five. I need him within the Order, something that wouldn't have happened if he was activated first as the hybrid. It will be different for the female twins, though. When their time comes, the younger twin needs to have her powers within the order activated before the older twin becomes a nightwalker, so they will both have their powers before turning. But the younger twin, the one with the blood of both a seventh daughter and a seventh son, will become a hybrid like you once she is changed by all three of you."

I stared at her, trying to understand everything she was saying. So much of her plan was being left up to chance.

"Who are you?" I demanded once again.

"In life, Adhamh was my husband. My name is Aoibh. The spell that created the first nightwalker and daywalker started with us. Cast by the leader of the coven that all members of the Order originated from, a man named Sithech." She laughed, though little humour was behind it.

"Adam and Eve?" My mind was reeling.

"That's right, the original Adam and Eve. Cast out of paradise when a snake tempted Eve with an apple. Sithech became Seth, a name often aligned with Satan or Lucifer. At least they cast him correctly in their little story." She smirked a little, but I couldn't see anything funny about any of this. *"Adhamh and I must be together when the time comes for this to end. And the steps that I have set in motion now will ensure that will happen. So you will be playing*

your part, Connor. Because you're tied to all of this now, whether you like it or not." And with those final words, she disappeared in a blur, leaving me standing alone alongside my brother's body, my brain a mess of questions and horror from what I had just learned.

I stayed there for the next seven days until Liam stirred, and then I slipped out into the night again.

How long was I to be expected to play this part? Adhamh could never know of this, or he would just kill me. But Aoibh had said it could be centuries. Something that I prayed was an exaggeration. Because with each moment I was exposed to this evil, it was harder to keep a hold of my human side.

I pushed Connor's arm away from me and leapt to my feet, needing to put distance between us while I processed everything I had just seen. I could feel my hands shaking, and I raked them through my hair, staring at him in shock. Connor watched while I began pacing, making no move to offer any further explanation.

"Eve set this all in motion? She told me she'd heard about the prophecy, but that memory...."

"Eve has been lying to so many people for centuries. I have no idea how she keeps track of it all. But she has manipulated this entire charade from the start. We are nothing more than her pawns in all of it." Connor's expression clouded over, and I had to remind myself again that he was not Liam, although that thought made me think of something Eve had revealed to Connor five hundred years ago.

"What the hell did she mean about you being created to be Liam's darker self?"

"Exactly what she said. Aurora and I exist purely so that you and Liam have the powers of the seventh son and daughter flowing through you. But because Aurora and I shared the same wombs, the magic from you guys passed to us. It's certainly been comforting to know that my entire existence came about so that my saintly younger brother gets to be the good guy. If I weren't already evil, that would have been enough to set it off," he said darkly.

"Quit trying to convince me that you are this evil being when you just confirmed that you are like me."

"I'm nothing like you, Isolde. That memory was five hundred years ago. I have spent five hundred years surrounded by creatures of the purest evil and expected to play my part. And I did. I played it well. I have killed. I have destroyed families. I've toyed with my brother countless times out of spite and anger. Do not fool yourself. I am not the tragic hero in all of this." Connor stalked towards me, stopping inches from my face and glaring at me.

"Is that why there is this pull between us? Because we're both hybrids?" I needed all the answers now, and this was the closest I'd come to learning the truth of who I was.

"I don't know. I feel a similar pull towards Aurora, and I imagine Liam has felt something as well, at least before her transition. Who knows, maybe it's because I'm literally Liam's other half." Connor laughed darkly.

I liked this theory. It made me feel marginally better about the fact that I seemed to be so attracted to my boyfriend's twin brother.

"That explains a lot." It also explained my memory of Aurora's inadvertently using fire magic.

"Of course, that's the answer that you cling to. Anything to deny the truth behind what is happening between us." Connor shook his head.

"Nothing is happening between us! I love Liam. Whatever this mess is between you and me, it means nothing!"

"It means everything! There was a connection when I first saw you in that university auditorium. I know you felt it - stop lying to yourself!" He gripped my shoulders and shook me slightly, but I shoved his hands away.

"I thought you were Liam!"

"You hadn't even met Liam yet!"

I didn't know who was angrier, but I stepped away from Connor again, needing to keep the distance between us in case it spiralled into another anger-fuelled kissing session.

"Stop trying to convince me you're the one I should be with, Connor. If I'm forced to choose, you know I will choose Liam."

Connor had been moving to close the space between us once more but came to an abrupt halt at my words. It was like the fight just fell out of him, and his expression closed over once again, the mask of evil settling over his features.

"If that is your decision, Isolde, then so be it. But know this - I have no intention of remaining Eve's puppet through all of this. Whatever her master plan is, I will be playing no part anymore. I chose this path for myself long ago, and I'll be damned if that witch will play me any further. I did what she needed. I made sure Adam was the one to turn your sister. I told him about the prophecy but left out a few important parts. As far as he knows, we failed. I ensured that Aurora and I didn't feed on you until Liam was in the room." His eyes flashed again while he glared at me. His jaw twitched, and I could tell he struggled to control his emotions.

"But I'm done now. So when we meet next, Isolde, all traces of my tortured soul will be gone, and you better believe you won't like what you see instead." With those words, he vanished, leaving me standing alone again after having yet more truths dumped on top of me.

I could feel so many emotions beginning to swirl inside me, the last few weeks of constant chaos threatening to overpower me.

I began to shake uncontrollably and felt something inside me snap. A burning sensation began to form in my chest.

My arms flung out wide, my head snapped back, and my entire body erupted, sending a fountain of flames soaring into the sky like some fiery bat signal.

Everything around me was ablaze, and I lost all control of the power that engulfed me.

A single thought flowed through my mind.

Let it all burn.

Epilogue

LIAM

I HAD SPENT THE night killing any nightwalkers I found in a failed attempt to work off the pent-up anger and frustration within me. When daylight arrived, and I was no closer to getting past it all, I had walked without a destination. I returned to the home that had once been my sanctuary but now felt empty and cold without Isolde.

I desperately needed a drink, and once I walked through the door, I made a beeline for the whiskey cabinet. I poured myself a glass and took both the bottle and the glass onto the balcony. Night had long since fallen, and I stared out at the view, the lights of the houses across the river in Bulimba twinkling away. Even with all I knew was occurring between Isolde and Connor, I needed to know she was safe. I regretted leaving her the way that I did.

But how was I meant to get past the fact that Isolde was drawn to my brother? The same brother who I had been fighting for the last five hundred years and was a creature of the purest evil? What did this mean of what Isolde had become? She was something different, and I felt sick knowing that it was my fault. I was meant to protect her, yet I had been coerced into turning her into something no one had anticipated. I needed to speak to Eve and force her to explain what Isolde had become.

I threw back my second glass of whiskey and began to pour my third when a flash of light in the distance drew my attention across the river. I could feel a burning sensation in my chest that I knew had nothing to do with the whiskey, and I watched a ball of flame shoot into the sky. I could think of only one thing that was causing that, and coupled with the burning in my chest, I knew immediately that Isolde was in danger.

I jumped to my feet, intent on reaching her as quickly as possible when a noise behind me caused me to turn around.

Damon stepped out of the shadows in front of me, closely followed by another man, and I was surprised that they had been able to keep their presence cloaked from me. That surprise turned to anger when the stranger raised his hand towards me, and my body seized up. Unable to move, I could do nothing to stop him when he came towards me, keeping me in place with his magic. He stopped in front of me and dropped his arm to his side, but whatever he had done kept me from being able to move from where I stood. I had never experienced magic like this before, and genuine fear began to pump through my veins for the first time in a long time.

"What are you doing, Damon?" I demanded, and he smirked at me from behind his companion.

"I thought surely Eve would have told you the truth by now. I shouldn't be surprised, though. She always did like to make things as dramatic as possible." He gestured towards the man beside him, who was surveying me closely.

"This is my father. You can call him Seth. We have a lot to discuss. But first, let me just do one thing." He reached forward and touched my forehead. I felt a sharp pain before falling into darkness.

If you have a moment

THANK YOU FOR READING! I hope you enjoyed Blood Memories. Stay tuned for The Order of the Dragon – Book III which will be available in early 2024.

Please take a moment to leave a rating or review on the platform you purchased from or Goodreads. Every review helps in an incredible way.

Acknowledgements

This series wouldn't be possible without the help of several people.

Firstly, to my sister, Melinda. Thank you for being my loudest cheerleader. I love that you're as into this journey as I am. From learning how to make reels, giving much-needed feedback as a beta reader, and attending book events with me, you have made these last few months much easier!

To my husband, Andrew, for accepting that I have become surgically attached to my laptop, sharing me with this imaginary world that has taken over my brain, and listening to me talk about vampires even more than ever before. Love you, baby!

To my friend and editor, Krystal, thank you for encouraging me to take the plunge into the writing world in the first place and answering all my questions about grammar, exposition and plot lines. Even with the time difference, you're always there when I need you!

To my friend and beta-reader, Jammi-Lee, thank you for your feedback, love for these characters, and for being one of my biggest cheerleaders!

To my friend, beta-reader and proofreader, Shannon, thank you for sitting through countless hours with me, working on covers, trying to get dimensions right, and finding all my errors!

Thank you to the friends and family who have cheered me on as I took the plunge and made this dream a reality. Your support has meant the world to me.

To my VA Book Club girlies, Jacquie, Megan, Mady, Ashley, and Jordan, thank you for talking books with me and for reading my book!

To the new friends that I've met since starting this journey, Alisha, Lauren, Demi, Mel, Kaitlyn, Amber, Jess and countless others from the Bookstagram and BookTok communities, thank you so much for all your advice and for making me feel so welcome. I never thought I'd find such a giving group of friends via social media.

And finally, to my daughter, Evelyn. You are my inspiration, the love of my life and the reason I decided to finally pursue my dream of becoming an author. I hope seeing Mummy so happy inspires you to pursue your dreams and helps you see you can be whatever and whoever you want to be when you grow up.

About the Author

Allison A. Andrews is a wife and mother of one based in Brisbane, Australia.

Having always been an avid reader with an overactive imagination, when she isn't writing, she loves spending time with family and friends, travelling the world, and dreaming of the next story she can tell.

Website: https://www.allisonaandrews.com/

Also By

Illusions – Order of the Dragon Book I